SPIRITS AND SPELLS

Warlocks MacGregor

MICHELLE M. PILLOW

Michelle M. Pillow® - MichellePillow.com

About Spirits and Spells

Charlotte Carver is going insane—suffering with everything from memory loss, to hallucinations, to phantom conversations she can't recall having. Something tells her it's not a coincidence that it all started when the MacGregor family moved to town, and the one person who knows what's going on is the last person Charlotte would ask for help. Her new landlord, Niall MacGregor, is not the most approachable man but that hasn't stopped the brooding Scottish biker from invading her dreams.

Motorcycle riding werewolf, Niall MacGregor is the longtime supernatural enforcer for his warlock family. He has regretted more than a few things he's done in the name of duty, but taking Charlotte's memories is the biggest. It was necessary, to both protect the family and save Charlotte's sanity. But the intimate glimpse into her mind has only made him want things he can never have—including the gorgeous, brave woman herself.

When luck finds Charlotte's memories returning, her attraction to Niall explodes, thrusting her into a magickal world. There is little time to adjust as another of Niall's past regrets has come back to threaten everything they hold dear.

Warning: Contains yummy, hot, mischievous MacGregors who are almost certainly up to no good on their quest to find true love.

Warlocks MacGregor® Series

SCOTTISH MAGICKAL WARLOCKS

Love Potions

Spellbound

Stirring Up Trouble

Cauldrons and Confessions

Spirits and Spells

Kisses and Curses

Magick and Mischief

A Dash of Destiny

Night Magick

More Coming Soon

Visit www.MichellePillow.com for details.

Note from the Author

The term "warlock" is a variation on the Old English word "waerloga," primarily used by the Scots. It meant traitor, monster, deceiver, or other variations. The MacGregor Clan does not look at themselves as being what history has labeled their kind. To them, warlock means magick, family, and immortality. This book is not meant to be a portrayal of modern day witches or those who have such beliefs. The MacGregors are a magickal class all their own.

As with all my books, this is pure fantasy. In real life, please always practice safe sex and magic(k).

Author recommends reading the books in order of release.

To stay informed about when a new book is released sign up for updates:

michellepillow.com/author-updates

To Kelli Collins an awesome editor who helped this MacGregor make his deadline. Also, Uncle Raibeart has a proposal for you. Trust me, you should just go ahead and tell him no.

Chapter One

Green Vallis, Wisconsin

"They're a cult."

The distorted words hung in the musty air like sagging cobwebs, but Charlotte Carver heard them as clearly as she felt the damp air on her skin. They sounded like they came from an old record player that had seen better days. And to make things even spookier, they were whispered in *her* voice.

Her memory had been shoddy as of late, to say the least, but she was sure that she would remember having a conversation about cults. She looked around and was able to discern from the stone foundation that she was in a basement. The dusky light seemed to drain color from her surroundings.

Charlotte felt the texture of a rope against her hand and glanced down. Her fingers were empty. She felt heavy, like her legs were made of lead. The notion that she wouldn't be able to move very far if she tried haunted her, almost to paralysis.

"They're going to sacrifice us," her raspy voice continued against pops and scratches of the record. Water dripping into a puddle somewhere only added to the eerie ambiance. *"We have to get out of here."*

"I don't understand," Charlotte said. None of this made sense.

"We don't know that." Lydia Barratt was her best friend. She knew that voice better than her own, even as the recording warped it. No, it was Lydia MacGregor now.

"Lydia?" Charlotte called. "Are you there? What is this place? What are we hearing?"

"I heard them. When they brought me here, they told me my sacrifice would be appreciated. They're sick." Again, Charlotte knew her own voice, but had no memory of the conversation.

"Hello, anyone? What is this place?" she yelled at the top of her lungs. "What is happening?"

"Ya don't need to be here," a man responded, much calmer than her voice had been.

She recognized the Scottish accent of Niall MacGregor, her landlord, and the brother of Lydia's new husband. His words were stronger, clearer than the recording. What was he doing here, in this basement from a black and white horror movie with her?

Niall made her nervous. Hell, he could make anyone nervous. He had a commanding presence that filled a room, even when he didn't say a word.

Sometimes, when he looked at her, she felt as if she would be less exposed if she were standing naked in front of a hundred people. Not that Niall had ever seen her naked. That was just how confident his knowing gaze was.

Charlotte searched her surroundings, looking for him. The room was empty.

Light streaming through a small window revealed an old furnace and water heater in the corner. Next to it were some wooden stairs leading out of the basement. Charlotte tried to go toward them. "Lydia, are you down here? I see a way out."

Suddenly, iron bars fell from the ceiling, blocking off the exit. Charlotte covered her ears as the clanging of metal on the stone floor rang around the small basement. The impact shook the ground and reverberated up through the floor and her legs, shaking every part of her. She looked up and down in a panic. The bars only fortified her fear that she was being held captive in the torture chamber of a house of horrors.

"This door does not exist within ya anymore," Niall said. His green eyes appeared first out of the shadows, bright in color but lacking the teasing light common to the other men in his family. His brown hair fell to his chin, and she had the impression that it was more out of neglect than a style choice. His kilt looked well worn. For a man from a wealthy family, he seemed to go out of his way to look like he didn't come from money. Still, on the surface, he was handsome, rugged, and moody. Whenever he came to Green Vallis, he drew attention like a movie star bad boy, riding into town on his motorcycle, returning from some mysterious adventure.

None of these things impressed Charlotte, for they were surface dressing. All the MacGregor men were handsome. If she was interested in a pretty face, there were several single ones to choose from—Euann and Rory were both sweet and amiable, dressed in designer clothing, and appeared to like having a good time. And they smiled at her. Niall never smiled.

Like now. He was definitely not smiling as he looked at her. "Ya do not want to go beyond this room."

"But..." She pointed at the door, only to see it disappear. Water dripped again, a solitary ambiance that caused the dread inside of her to intensify.

"And ya do not need these bars, or these windows," he said. "Ya do not need this night. Let it go, Charlotte."

"Where's Lydia?" She looked around. Panic filled her. None of this was as it should be. "I heard her. Where is she? I have to find her."

Charlotte ran to the window and grabbed hold of the sill. Her fingers felt the strain as she pulled herself up before bracing her toes in the stone foundation to hold a precarious position. Outside, she saw Lydia's lawn.

That's weird.

Lydia owned an old Victorian house, and her basement looked nothing like the one Charlotte was currently inside.

A blue light flashed past where she looked and she gasped, almost slipping. She held on tighter. Lightning flashed across the landscape, blowing tree limbs over like toothpicks across the grass, as a windstorm raged.

"Ya cannot keep coming back here, Charlotte," Niall said from behind her. "Leave it buried. Stop digging."

A demonic creature's face appeared in the window. Charlotte cried out as she lost her grip. She fell back, unable to look away. It was half man, half panther, and one hundred percent terrifying. His eyes glowed like embers and his sharp fangs glistened in the dark as, behind him, lightning struck closer than before. A clawed hand pressed to the glass, lighting it up with an ominous, foreboding glow.

"*Let us out!*" her recorded voice yelled, but no sound would come from her trembling lips.

"I told ya to stop looking." Niall appeared before her, blocking the creature in the window. He reached out as if to touch her. "I would take it all back if I could. I would rewind time. I—"

Charlotte gasped and flung her arms as she came out of a deep sleep, trying to swat the invisible hand that pulled away from her cheek. It took a moment to realize she fought a dream that wasn't there. The smell of a basement stayed with her as she turned on the mattress. Eventually, her breathing evened itself out.

Her empty bedroom held very little; one could say it had a minimalist's touch—a lavender-scented candle left burning too long, a crumpled paperback discarded when she fell asleep, and a butcher knife on her nightstand. She vaguely remembered putting the knife there, but it wasn't the first time her tired mind had felt the need to protect itself by rejecting reality.

The silence of downtown streets below resonated with a shiver that ran up her spine. For a moment, she second-guessed the glow of the street-lights that fell across her bed, imagining the shadow of a spidery creature. The hour was late and here she was again in the arms of insomnia. Sadly, she hadn't slept a full night in a long time. In fear, she gazed wearily at the window as if expecting there to be something or someone outside the glass, standing two stories tall looking in on her, waiting for the right time to reach inside.

The whisper of the voice still lingered, but the images leading up to it faded before she could hold on to them. *"I would take it all back if I could. I would rewind time."*

"Take it all back," she whispered, unable to recall what the words might have referred to.

There are aches that cannot be described, pains that settle in the stomach and chest caused by nothing more than a faded memory. Charlotte knew there was something she should recall, like a scary movie she watched through her fingers as a child—but its plot she could no longer recall. She remembered the feeling though, the unfounded fear. It crept in every time she closed her eyes.

There was something she needed to remember.

Why couldn't she remember?

Charlotte closed her eyes, trying to start at the beginning.

She recalled her childhood clearly. It had been no better or worse than most people's. She remembered Buck Mitchell pinching her backside when they were eight because his older brother dared him to. She'd tied his pants to a flagpole and gave him a wedgie, trying to lift him off the ground in retaliation. Buck learned to respect women a little more after that.

Charlotte remembered when her best friend Lydia asked her to come to work for her in her home-based business, Love Potions, after Lydia's grandmother had died. Annabelle Barratt raised

Lydia after her parents died. She might not have been Charlotte's grandmother, but she had been a great influence in her life. Gramma Annabelle had believed in the old magick, not silly magic tricks, but actual magick. She'd taught Lydia and Charlotte that there were things in the universe that could not be explained. She believed there were those who could harness a deep power and control the earth and sky.

Annabelle had sometimes gone off the deep end and had tried to teach them vampire lore, protection spells to ward off evil, and how to avoid stepping into fairy rings, as if those topics had a practical application in everyday life.

Annabelle might have been crazy in some regards, but she'd gotten one thing right. Ghosts were real. Charlotte had seen them, and could rationalize that people transferred their energy into the ether when they died. It also explained why so many people believed in haunting in the modern day. However, Charlotte did not believe in vampires and fairies. If creatures went around entrancing humans and drinking their blood, someone would have surely noticed.

Annabelle was a green witch, a naturalist, which was just another way of saying she was a hippie without the patchouli. She had taught them about herbs and natural remedies. Now Charlotte helped Lydia make teas, candles, lotions, and bath products. Hanging out with her friend all day for work, what could be better than that? It was a dream job.

All that she remembered. Those memories were clear.

Then the new, rich neighbors bought the house on the hill—an old mansion that no one in Green Vallis could afford to upkeep. Like everyone else, Charlotte had been charmed by the MacGregors with their Scottish accents, charismatic ways, and love of kilts... at first. Now she didn't completely trust them. The feeling of dread she couldn't shake, and her sensation of missing time, both came soon after their arrival. The family was swallowing her hometown whole, buying up property and weaving themselves into the fabric of the small town as if they had always been there.

A MacGregor had even purchased her apartment building. She balled her hand into a fist, thinking of Niall. Like his brothers and cousins— heck, even like the older MacGregor generation— he was more handsome than any man had a right to be, but he was also grumpy and arrogant, and...

Why couldn't she remember? It was right there, on the tip of her lips.

Charlotte felt a tap on her leg and jerked up on the bed. A dark spot wet the knee of her pajama pants. She frowned, instantly looking at the ceiling. Water came through her light fixture and had been dripping on her while she slept. It soaked her leg and her bedspread. She rolled off the mattress with a grimace and glared upward. This apartment used to be her sanctuary. Now it seemed to be falling apart around her.

"Freaking MacGregors," she grumbled.

Pushing the wet pajama pants down her legs, she kicked them aside and grabbed a pair of skinny jeans from the floor and pulled them on. She hopped and wiggled, tugging them up her hips so she could button them.

Charlotte frowned as the water continued to drip on her bed. It quickly became a steady stream. She grabbed the pajama pants and tried to soak up the mess.

Suddenly, a rush of soapy dishwater dumped down onto her. She gasped and scrambled off the bed. The brief waterfall slowed back to a trickle, but the damage had been done. Her mattress was ruined, the ceiling was bowed and cracked, and the light fixture was wet.

Tears of frustration filled her eyes. It was difficult enough trying to sleep without the added bonus of disgusting ceiling water falling on her from the apartment above. All she wanted was to have a normal life back where her biggest concern was too many internet lotion orders.

Chapter Two

Niall MacGregor took a deep breath as he rode his motorcycle down the quiet sides streets of his new hometown. The purr of the hog's engine reverberated through the handlebars he gripped as he leaned into a corner while rolling back the throttle of the customized all-black Harley Sportster. Niall's customization of the bike barely resembled the factory version of the classic, not to mention Euann's mods using the infamous MacGregor magick.

Some of the brick roads had been paved over with concrete, so there were patches of white over the red. He was careful not to rev his engine too loudly, not wanting to disturb those sleeping within the uniform houses of the small-town neighborhood.

The moonlight tingled on his skin each time he passed from under a tree canopying the street. The wolf inside him responded to moonlight, stirring as if to remind Niall that it was there. But after three centuries, he had well learned to control the monster within. His warlock powers kept the wolf locked up tight until it was safe to let it roam free.

The MacGregors had only been in Green Vallis, Wisconsin, for a short time, but they already owned nearly a quarter of the town's commercial property. The vast MacGregor empire kept growing with each new acquisition. It took all of them to keep the family business in order.

The family had picked Green Vallis for several reasons. First, because the old mansion on the hill overlooking the town was practical since so many of them lived in the area. Some outlandish Englishman had built the mansion, and it was too large for any of the locals to maintain so it had sat empty for years. Second, the surrounding nature would fuel their magick and their spirits. Third, there was a special power here, beneath the ground in the convergence of ley lines. However, since ley lines created a surge of energy for the supernatural, it also acted as a beacon of fuel to non-warlocks, which accounted for the surge in family troubles lately.

By nature, the MacGregor warlocks were lusty creatures who thrived on sexual energy. Sex gave a brief surge of power to their magick. If a warlock were lucky enough to find his *fíorghrá*, his *true love*, he'd be powerful indeed. Niall didn't believe he had a *fíorghrá*. True love was a blessing, and he had done and seen too much in his long life to think he deserved such happiness.

It wasn't as if Niall didn't believe in love. He did. His brothers, Erik and Iain, had found love, and he was happy for both men. Plus, his parents had been married for hundreds of years.

The clan elders—who consisted of his parents, uncles and aunts—used to press the matter with their children but had finally given up. The only way Niall would find someone was if he cast a spell to make it happen. But then, that wouldn't work either. Erik had said something profound about it once, "Love couldn't be forced or else it wasn't love."

Each warlock had his own special abilities and curse. Niall had been born a wolf shifter. They said it was why he was so fiercely protective of his family, and why he could never be tamed. No one could explain to him why the wolf was such a dominant part of his genetics, but then, sometimes magick was hard to explain.

Currently, his siblings Euann and Malina, and his cousin Rory, lived in the mansion, along with his parents Angus and Margareta, Uncle Murdoch and Aunt Cait, and crazy Uncle Raibeart. Other members of the family came and went. It sounded like a lot, but the twenty thousand square foot house had sixty or so rooms in it. There was plenty of space for several dozen MacGregors to move in. The elders had an area to practice their magick while maintaining separate offices to work out of.

His brother Iain stayed in the apartment above his wife Jane's greenhouse and nursery. The oldest, Erik, lived in the only other house on the estate with his wife, Lydia.

Niall always kept a separate apartment close to the family, but away enough that they couldn't monitor all his comings and goings. Mischievousness ran in the MacGregor bloodline. Pranks and misfired spells were never in short supply. He supposed living for hundreds of years affected even the most serious of warlocks. They had to do something to ease the boredom of centuries. Regardless if they lived in the mansion or elsewhere in the town, one thing remained true: MacGregors always stayed together, since their early days in the barbaric Scottish countryside.

At least Niall's role as a hunter kept him from having to run a family corporation. It was the one plus he could think of to his job. All he was expected to do was manage the apartment building he lived in downtown. He had no use for business meetings and small talk.

In that way, he missed the days long past, when they could live in vast private estates and no one dared to question the noble families. If they were exposed, they would simply move, or deny the accusation. But now, in the age of internet and broadcasts, security cameras and cell phone pictures, hiding what they were became that much harder and that much more important. If they were exposed, the whole world could tune in to watch. In a small town like Green Vallis, it was easier to control perception. Worldwide exposure could not be contained so easily. The last time mortals learned of shifters and warlocks, they started the witch trials. The 1590 North Berwick trials nearly killed his sister, and did kill his aunt. Mortals always feared them, instantly believing anything supernatural had to be evil.

Yes, there was evil in the world, but it wasn't limited to the supernatural. Niall and his kin were simply a magickal family—immortal, powerful, and trying to survive the centuries in peace.

Euann would argue that technology and science were their friends. Humans began to think logically and thus could explain away magick as folklore and myth. Superstitions were replaced by accepted facts. The rise of magicians and their fake magic tricks gave the illusion that old magick wasn't real. Those annoying habits humans had to ward off supposed evil, like runes to divine the future and painting blood symbols over their doorways, had all but disappeared and made it easier for warlocks to roam a little more freely.

If only humans were their biggest threat. Sure, humans were dangerous in unified numbers, but there was so much more happening in the world than the mortals knew. Dark forces roamed the earth, eager to tempt with sultry promises. For Niall's wolf, these were promises of wild, unfettered freedom to do whatever it wanted. Niall kept a tight leash on the animal within.

He felt the vibration of the motor between his

legs and grinned, wanting to go faster. He let the bike pick up speed for a few blocks before forcing himself to slow once more. If he had his choice tonight, he would have kept riding straight out of town. But, he never had his choice. He went where duty demanded, and tonight it demanded he ride back to his apartment, where some of his family waited for him.

The MacGregor clan was really pulling out all the supernatural fuckups this time. He came back from a hunt to find his new hometown the center of magickal headaches. Malina's husband the luck demon had apparently crawled his way back from the dead, bringing with him a run of bad luck.

If Niall didn't figure out how to clear the MacGregor mansion of ghosts, goblins, gremlins, fairies, and who knew what else, his apartment building was no longer going to afford him privacy. Of late, it had become a haven for several members of the family after they'd fled the supernatural infestations of the mansion on the hill.

What he wouldn't give for one night of normal. He had just ridden back into town after dealing with a leprechaun outbreak in the Midwest—they'd been creating small earthquakes in Oklahoma and Kansas—only to find Malina's husband, Dar, causing havoc. He originally thought he'd gotten lucky when the leprechauns simply vanished, but then discover them running amuck in the MacGregor gardens. Before leprechauns, it was a vampire nest. Before vampires, it was chupacabras in Puerto Rico, boggarts in Europe, a very hairy human people thought was an actual Bigfoot, a lizard man in the Louisiana swamps claiming to be a dragon shifter from another planet, and a water spirit poking holes in the bottom of gondolas in Venice. Before those it had been a rogue werewolf in the Carpathian Mountains. He'd nearly died in Romania. And no one in his family even knew.

Niall loved his sister, but Malina's reckless decisions were what led him to this moment. In the sixties, she had fallen in love with and married a luck demon while partying in Las Vegas. Dar could give good or bad luck as he saw fit, changing people's fates on a whim. It had been Niall's duty to send all demons back to hell. That's what hunters did. They sent demons back to hell, rampaging vampires into eternal rest, and fairyland creatures through the veil to their own world. Niall always did what he was supposed to.

Somehow, Dar had survived the trip to his fiery tomb and came looking for revenge in the form of some extremely bad luck for the MacGregor family. Thus, the MacGregor mansion now overrun with supernatural problems.

Niall dealt with all the things no one else wanted or were able to. When his family was in trouble, they called him. When there was an unpleasant task, it fell on his shoulders. And he always did what had to be done...like wiping the memories of a poor young woman who had seen too much.

Charlotte Carver.

Niall's motorcycle weaved as he swerved to avoid a parked car. The mere thought of Charlotte had that effect on him, so he tried to block his mind from thinking of her. Though, it was difficult when they lived in the same building. Her beauty was undeniable, even if the feral light in her brown eyes was a constant reminder of her delicate state.

Charlotte and her best friend, Lydia Barratt, had been attacked by two shadow creatures known as *lidércs*. They were like incubi, using vessels to draw power. In this case, they'd used Charlotte and Lydia to try to steal Iain and Erik's magick.

Lydia's rare genetic makeup made her an *inthrall*, a perfect vessel for one particular warlock —Erik. It gave her a natural link to him that allowed her to borrow his magick. The fact that Lydia was Erik's *fíorghrá*, his one true love, made their situation unique. Lydia had survived the attack with her sanity intact.

However, Charlotte was not so lucky. She was not Iain's *inthrall* or *fíorghrá*. The *lidérc* had forced her to drink a potion that made her a conduit to suck Iain's power. A warlock's power was his very essence, his soul. Taking it had been excruciating for Charlotte.

Niall hadn't been there, but he knew every detail as if he'd been standing beside her while it happened. It had been his duty to erase her memory of the event. Considering the state that the incident had left her in, it was the best they could do for her. Mortals talked tough, but the truth was most were not mentally equipped to carry the knowledge of the supernatural. If the creatures themselves didn't drive them to insanity, knowing none of their friends and family would believe them often did. Charlotte didn't remember that real magick existed in the world, and it was best to keep it that way.

When Niall had gone into Charlotte's memories to pull the bad ones, he'd seen more than he should have. He'd felt who she was, saw her secrets, absorbed her fears, and witnessed her doubts. She'd marked him deeply, and it was as if, by taking her memories, he'd somehow left a part of himself inside of her, and he couldn't get it back.

It was more than a mere attraction to her. Of course he was physically tempted. She was a stunningly beautiful woman with a great smile and heartfelt laugh. Yet, that didn't matter. There wasn't anything he could do about his attraction toward her but keep it a secret, and hope that it went away. As for the piece he'd lost to her, he would have to make himself forget about it. Charlotte deserved more than he could give.

He'd taken Charlotte's nightmares as his own and had been haunted by them ever since. They churned inside of him with the rest of the bad memories he carried. But, if he hadn't, she'd have gone insane. He'd seen it before. She had been touched by too much magick. Humans were so fragile.

Sensing his aunt Cait was about to call, he pulled over to the side of the road and reached for his phone. It started ringing in his hand. He shut off the bike and answered, "Aye?"

"Where are ya?" Cait asked, her tone rushed.

"In town." He glanced over the quiet street and

focused on a house. Niall no longer bothered to imagine what a normal human life inside a normal family home might look like.

"I know there is much happening tonight, but ya need to keep a closer eye on Charlotte. I have a feeling." Cait did not need to explain more. Warlocks trusted their feelings.

Niall sighed in exasperation. "I moved next to her in the apartment building, what else would ya have me do, Cait? Crawl into her bed and pretend to be a pillow?"

Well, that was stupid. He really didn't need to be picturing what it would be like to lay in Charlotte's bed.

"Take that tone again with me, lad, and I'll find a spell to make that happen," Cait warned. As an elder, she believed herself entitled to respect. However, at three hundred and sixty-some years old, Niall wasn't a child to be scolded anymore.

"Charlotte is well in hand," Niall answered. "Euann, Malina, Rory, and Uncle Raibeart are in my apartment, and I'm heading back now to rejoin them." He paused, as a thought struck him. "Is there any particular reason you're calling me about this again, besides a general feeling of unease? Has more happened while I was away? I thought ya said

Malina was able to stop her sleepwalking episodes. It's the middle of the night, she should be sleeping."

Euann's security cameras had caught footage of Charlotte standing on Lydia's front lawn in the middle of the night for three hours, simply staring at the road like she was under a trance and unable to move.

"Please tell me no one tried to take more memories out of the lass," Niall said with a frown. Erasing one event was relatively safe under normal circumstances, but Charlotte had suffered a serious magickal trauma, one that no person should have to live with. Time could fill in some gaps in a person's memory, but create too many holes and it became impossible for the mind to recover.

"There was a strong disruption," Cait answered, and he imagined she was fiddling with her string of pearls as she spoke. "It is easy to be distracted with that Dar on the loose, but we need to keep an eye on her so Charlotte does not become Helena."

"We have learned much since Helena." Niall wished his family would stop bringing the past into this. He had never meant to hurt Helena, and did not appreciate the reminder of his failure. "Times are different now. I am not that man."

"Stop mumbling, I can't hear ya over this cackling," Cait said. "I think the *gremain* I petrified is starting to thaw. Just keep an eye out, is all I'm saying. That one's sanity is unstable."

Cait hung up. Niall slipped the phone into his pocket and started the engine to continue home. He told himself that tonight was just like any other. The threats were no more or less than what he'd faced a thousand times before. *Gremains* and fairies, leprechauns and demons, he could easily go up against an army of them. Yet the thought of failing Charlotte terrified him.

Niall had broken her to save her from a much worse fate. He carried the burden of her fate inside of him. All that pain and fear she'd felt was now his, as was the unreturned feelings churning in his heart like a hurricane on a magickal leash. Charlotte would never know the truth, not if he had anything to say about it.

Chapter Three

Charlotte scrubbed the wet floor, trying to rid it of the smell of dishwater. Tears of frustration filled her eyes. All she wanted was a full night's sleep in a dry, comfortable bed, and her sanity back. It wasn't like she asked for the sun, the moon, and the stars, wrapped up in a million dollars.

Seeing a piece of scrap paper under the bed, she pulled it out. The scribbles looked like her handwriting but she didn't remember writing it.

"They're out there," Charlotte read, having a hard time deciphering a few of the words. "No eyes in the bag. No...breathing? Darkness. Basement dark. Drink the burning. Choke it down. Pain when it comes in. Remember they want you to have an extra soul but will rip it out when..." The rest was an illegible series of lines, but for some reason she felt like she knew what it was trying to say. "I can feel it in my bones, eating, chewing, crunching. They want to make me forget, but I see what they're doing. I see. They can't have my soul. I hid it where they will never find it."

A tear slipped down her cheek. She wadded up the crazy ramblings and shoved them into the water bucket to hide the evidence. Why was this happening? She was a rational person. She didn't walk around believing that souls could be ripped out and hidden. In fact, she didn't consider souls much at all. Now, ghosts, she knew those were real. She supposed those could be souls, but...

Dripping water broke her concentration and she looked up in time to see another gush of dishwater pump down from the ceiling.

"Oh, come on!" she yelled up at her upstairs neighbors in frustration. Sleeping was hard enough, and now she didn't even have a bed.

The temptation to give up, crawl into a corner, and never move again was strong. Maybe it was time she accepted the fact there was nothing physically wrong with her. Maybe this was all in her head. Maybe she was crazy. But it wasn't in her nature to give up. She needed to concentrate on what she could control.

Charlotte pushed up from the floor and went toward the window. She peered out at the shadowed red brick streets of downtown Green Vallis. The benches and sidewalks were empty. That wasn't unusual for the middle of the night. Streetlights flickered and dimmed as if their power fluctuated before becoming stronger. Seeing Niall's motorcycle, she gave a small growl of anger. He must have come home while she'd been cleaning.

Charlotte didn't care how late it was. She'd been leaving endless messages about the slow drip coming from her ceiling. This was unacceptable. She grabbed a flannel shirt and jerked it over her cami top, buttoning it as she marched out of her apartment and down the hall to where Niall stayed when he was in town.

She pounded on his door and then leaned her ear close to listen. The anger bubbling inside of her felt wonderful compared to the fear and uncertainty. She grabbed hold of that feeling, letting it overtake her reasoning.

When he didn't answer, she pounded harder and called out, "Hey, slumlord, I know you're in there. I saw your motorcycle outside, and I'm not leaving until you talk to me."

This time she heard movement and the low sound of voices. She straightened her shoulders and crossed her arms over her chest as she waited for him to open the door.

Instead of Niall, she came face to face with his more sociable brother. Euann had a constant playfulness in his solid brown eyes. His dark brown hair looked as if he'd been running his fingers through it. He gave her a flirtatious wink and said, "Hello, love. I was just thinking about ya."

She didn't believe him. Euann always had a pretty smile for her. However, she noticed it became brighter whenever his cousin Rory was around. Any flirting they did with her was more of a competition between the two of them than out of an attraction to her. When she'd met him, she thought there might be something there, but the feelings never developed beyond a passing flirtation that ended in friendly banter.

As expected, she saw Rory standing behind Euann with a grin. The night she'd met the two of them was the first instance where she'd forgotten time. Though to be fair, they had all been on the roof of the mansion drinking whiskey and scotch, and she could have just passed out.

"Oh, ah, hey, Euann," Charlotte acknowledged, trying to calm her anger so it wasn't misdirected at the wrong MacGregor. She tried to peek past him into the room but he leaned to block her view. "Is your brother here?"

"I like what you've done with your hair." Euann didn't step aside. He was completely unfazed by the fact she'd been screaming like a mad woman while pounding the door. He gave a pretend shiver, and said, "Fiery!"

"Uh, thanks." Charlotte automatically reached to touch the hair still piled into a messy bun on the top of her head. She'd fallen asleep with it tied up. On a whim, she had colored her naturally brown hair a deep red. She tried to push a wayward lock away from her face, but it instantly fell back down. Too aggravated to worry about how she looked, she asked, "Where's that slumlord brother of yours?"

"Hello, Charlotte." Niall's tone was stern, but then, when was it not? The man always sounded like whatever he was doing was the most serious thing on the planet. "What can I do for ya?"

She stepped forward, forcing Euann back as she stood in the doorway of Niall's apartment.

"The point of having a phone to leave messages on is to actually check the messages so your tenants can get ahold of you when shit goes wrong in your crappy building." She gestured to her wet jeans as evidence.

"This is not a slum. I live here, too," Niall countered.

Barely, she thought in irritation. The man was never home. Lights were going out in the hallways, the laundry room in the basement had a strange smell, and the security doors didn't appear too secure, since a stranger was able to get in and knock on her door earlier in the day.

"I've been calling for a month," she said in exasperation. "That makes you a slumlord."

She glanced around his apartment. Of course, he didn't have water leaking onto *his* furniture.

Euann and Niall's sister, Malina, stood near a couch. The furniture was practically the only decoration in the place beside a small dining table and wooden chairs. Niall didn't live like he came from a wealthy family. Or maybe he did...somewhere else.

Malina gave her a tight smile. The woman had the dark hair, eyes, and attitude of a MacGregor, but when she spoke, her accent sounded more British than Scottish. Tonight, she didn't look like her normally put-together self. She wore a faded T-shirt advertising the best tacos in the Midwest and baggy sweatpants, neither of which were her size. Charlotte had never seen Malina out of designer clothes.

Charlotte wondered what they were all doing here this late at night. Niall's family rarely came to the building. Euann and Rory smiled, but there was something off about the way they looked at her. She couldn't place it, and maybe she imagined it, but she had the distinct impression she'd interrupted something.

"What can I do for ya, Charlotte?" Niall asked when she merely stared at the apartment. "I'm a little busy tonight."

She frowned. He dared to get irritated with her? She was the one sleeping under water.

Charlotte had tried being nice. She'd tried being firm. She'd tried begging. At this point, she didn't care who heard her. "Oh, let's see. You can fix the drainpipe in my ceiling that you promised was taken care of before I drown. You can tell the people in the apartment above me to stop running their dishwasher until it's fixed, because they keep telling me they're not but I can hear it, and I get flooded with their dirty dishwater through my bedroom ceiling light fixture. I can't keep up with the buckets when I'm working the two jobs I have to have to pay for this overpriced place. And you can replace my mattress because it's ruined. *And* you can pay for the chiropractor visit I'm going to need after sleeping on a lumpy couch for too much longer."

There. Let his family hear how bad of a landlord he was.

"I promise it will be taken care of first thing tomorrow," Niall said calmly, as if he were the reasonable one in the conversation. How could she keep yelling if he didn't rise to the bait? "Anything else?"

Under her breath, she muttered, "I swear, I don't know how you are related to my best friend's husband." Charlotte turned to go but then thought better of it. "Yeah, there *is* another thing. Fix the security on the front and back entrances. I don't need gangster-looking guys at my door asking questions about you. If you're in deep with a bookie, then that's your business. I don't want that nonsense coming at me. I have enough to do." She gave a small wave at the others standing in the apartment. "It's great seeing you all again. Have a nice night."

Charlotte jerked the door closed before any of them could answer her.

"Gangsters? What the—" She heard Euann ask.

Charlotte took a deep breath, feeling only slightly better for having yelled at Niall. Her limbs shook with irritation. How could Niall just sit there all calm like she was the irrational one for wanting a dry bed?

Not for the first time, she thought about moving. Lydia was married now to Erik MacGregor, so his family was constantly popping up at work. MacGregors were in her apartment building. They were taking over several businesses in town. They were buying real estate. MacGregors were everywhere. Soon Green Vallis would probably have to change its name to MacGregorville.

Things would never be the way they were before—just two best friends making lotions and teas in a small Wisconsin town where nothing spectacular ever happened. She used to think the town was boring. Now she'd give anything to have things back the way they were.

Perhaps blaming the MacGregors for her current medical problems was wrong. How could they really be responsible for migraines and blackouts and lost time? But it was easier to blame them than admit the doctors didn't know how to fix her. She couldn't even admit the seriousness of the situation to herself, let alone tell anyone about it. Not even Lydia knew the full truth.

She started walking down the hall but stopped when the man who'd come by her apartment earlier in the day walked around the corner. He wore a suit that belonged in a 1950s Hollywood thug movie. He smiled when he saw her and opened his mouth to speak.

Charlotte held up her hand to stop him. It was taking everything in her not to cry in frustration. The man arched a brow. She turned and opened Niall's door without knocking. "Speaking of book-ies, here's Mr. 1950s Mobster now." Then to the man in the hall, she added, "Don't bother knocking at my door again. He's in here."

"Dar," Malina and Niall said loudly in unison. Charlotte stiffened at the sound, not understanding.

"Charlotte, get away from the door," Niall commanded.

Before she knew what was happening, he had ahold of her arm and was trying to pull her into his home. She yelped in surprise and swatted at him.

Niall tossed her behind him and she landed on his couch. "Stay there."

Charlotte instantly stood and began to protest. Malina ran toward the door as if to slam it, but the stranger pushed his way inside. Malina stumbled back. Whatever this was, Charlotte did not want to be involved. Niall tried to stop her from leaving by reaching for her arm.

"Don't touch me." This was the last straw. Charlotte was moving out of the building, perhaps the town. She couldn't take it. She literally felt herself going crazy.

"Charlotte, don't." Malina's tone was soft, but still commanding. Charlotte swung her arm out of Malina's reach when the woman tried to grab hold of her.

"What's wrong, doll face? Don't you want to introduce me to your friends?" The man in the doorway purposefully knocked into Charlotte as she tried to move past him. It was a light bump, but enough to cause her to stumble. She fell against the doorframe and he automatically reached out to keep her from falling. His touch was light, but it sent a tingling sensation over her shoulder to her neck and head.

Not again, Charlotte thought as she felt herself growing weaker.

"Let go of her!" Euann's voice sounded distant. There were a series of strange thumps, and it took her a moment to realize she could hear her heart beating. The noise sounded far away. She blinked as her vision blurred. People kept talking, but she couldn't make out all the words.

"Dar, let her go," Malina insisted. "She's human. She has nothing to do with us. She's fragile."

"Human?" Charlotte repeated. Had she heard that right? She looked at the man holding her arm. Dar? Maybe he would help her. "I don't feel well."

"Just a bit of bad luck," Dar told her. "It would appear I have extra tonight."

And then again, maybe not. Energy flowed out of her into Dar.

"Reverse it." Niall held out his arm. "Ya don't want her. Ya want us. Take me instead."

"Is she gone? I'm sorry I'm such a ladies' magnet. They can't seem to stay away from me." Raibeart MacGregor came from the bathroom wearing a bathrobe. He was the uncle of the other MacGregors in the room, and, well, there was no other way to put it: the man was about fifty cards short of a fifty-two-card deck. He'd proposed to about every single woman in town. If any had said yes, the man clearly did not remember. Still, that didn't explain why his bare legs poked out from under the bottom of a robe, and why no one else appeared to be reacting to his sudden presence or outfit.

Charlotte's head tingled. Was she hallucinating a man in a bathrobe? She tried to pull her arm free, but her body didn't listen.

Raibeart frowned at no one in particular. "Oh, it's only crazy Charlotte. And who's this fella with her?"

Only crazy Charlotte?

Great, crazy Raibeart thought she was the loony one.

"Don't call her that," Euann said from where he sat on the floor against a wall. Why was Euann on the floor? "She's not crazy."

Charlotte opened her mouth to thank him. Out of all the MacGregor's, Euann and Rory had always been the nicest to her.

"Lad, when you've had your brains swirled, and your memories plucked as much as that lassie has, ya can't help but be crazy," Raibeart countered. "Now get your arse up and meet Charlotte's new beau. That's no way to greet company."

Charlotte felt something warm along her mouth. The taste of blood flavored her lips.

Dar turned her to face him. "What are you? You're not one of them, that much is clear."

Charlotte tried to make him understand, "Please, help me. I have blackouts and seizures. I need to get to the hospital."

"Seizures?" Niall demanded. "Since when?"

"She *is* a full human, isn't she?" Dar sounded surprised. His eyes strayed to where her nose bled.

Maybe none of this was real. It had to be another hallucination. She felt the energy that had been pulled out of her arm slowly returning and her mind began to clear.

"So, you're still messing with people's lives," Dar said in disgust. "What the hell did you do to this one? I barely touched her, which means she was unbalanced to begin with." His grip lightened and he slid his hand around her back as he began walking her away from the apartment. She heard him whisper, "Don't be frightened. Luck will be on your side." Before adding louder, "You must care about her if you're so worried about what I'll do to her. Does she have something of value in her memories that you want? Been digging around in there, have you?"

"I can't remember where I was," Charlotte whispered. She saw flashes of a dark basement and then a bonfire. She saw shadows dancing. They crept up the hallway walls, belonging to figures that were not there. The images teased her like a nightmare.

"Dar, you didn't come here for Charlotte," Malina said. "You came for me. I'm the one you're mad at."

"You're right about that, doll," he said. "This was not how I'd planned the evening to go. It would seem the ghosts tried to take more good luck than I wanted to give them and left me a little drier than I realized."

"I see ghosts, too," Charlotte whispered as he kept talking, her eyes staying on the shadowed figures around them. No one paid attention to her. Dar and the MacGregors yelled at each other, the sound growing chaotic. She felt the energy reversing as it pulled out of her. The hallway melted from around her until she was standing on someone's lawn. Voices chanted in the distance. She felt the heat of a fire on her skin. She wasn't well. These shadows weren't real.

"Let her go, demon," Malina demanded. "Can't you see that poor girl has had enough bad luck all on her own? She's got nothing left to feed you with. Give the girl some of my luck and let her go. There is no challenge in killing a human. Let Rory and Euann take care of her. Take me in her place. I give you my word, I will walk with you out of this building."

"Malina, no," Niall ordered. "Take me instead of Charlotte or my sister. I'm the one who dealt the final blow. It was my idea to attack ya."

"I don't understand what any of you are talking about. Will someone take me to the hospital?" Charlotte mumbled. She was growing weaker by the moment. They continued to ignore her.

"Not so final a blow, was it?" Dar laughed, yet he didn't sound happy. "But it did hurt like hell trying to crawl back into my charred skin."

They were talking gibberish to each other—demons crawling out of hell, damned luck, and plucking people's memories? It was like she had walked in on the tail end of a joke, a bad one. And the punchline just seemed to drag on and on. The drone of it dizzying as it was mortifying.

Dar kept a hold on her arm, jerking her around each time he moved. And then a surge of energy filled Charlotte, clearing her foggy mind and pulling her back from the edge of passing out. Her gaze met Malina's as her eyes rolled and then dulled. A faint glow lit the hand on her arm as if Dar somehow gifted her Malina's life force.

Charlotte inhaled sharply so she could ingest the sudden flow of energy. The shadows on the wall disappeared. Before she could speak, Dar flung her toward Niall's chest.

Niall held her tight as if scared she'd run away. The shock of his nearness took her by surprise and for a moment, she couldn't move as she looked up at him.

"Dammit, Malina!" Niall stared after his sister. Dar pulled Malina down the hallway. "Ya don't have to do this."

"Stop him," Rory demanded.

"Euann, take Charlotte. Don't let her leave." Niall thrust her from his chest into someone else. Euann hugged her possessively close as he began dragging her back into Niall's apartment. Behind them, the rustling of clothes and men grunting; the sound of a struggle in the hall faded until a slamming door killed it completely.

"Let go of me," Charlotte demanded. She felt stronger than she had in a long time. Her thoughts raced with newfound clarity. "What the hell is going on? Who is that guy?"

"Well, um..." Euann gave her a guilty look. "Ya are dreaming?"

Charlotte arched a brow. The scary thing was, she halfway believed him. Her mind was not to be trusted. She scratched her hand to make sure she was awake. She was. She felt the press of her nails.

"Would ya like something to drink, love?" Raibeart winked at her, and he *was* wearing a robe. That part had been real. Maybe she hadn't hallucinated any of it.

Charlotte glanced around the apartment. Raibeart and Euann avoided her gaze. "You all have exactly three seconds to tell me what is going on, or I'll...I'll...I'll do something so drastic you'll wish you were never born."

"That was an old friend of Malina's, messing around," Rory said. "No reason to be concerned."

"Like a game?" Charlotte asked.

"Sure," Euann said.

"He told me he was Niall's bookie," Charlotte said.

"Did he?" Rory avoided her direct gaze.

"Does Niall owe money? Is that why he

kidnapped Malina?" Charlotte automatically felt her pockets for her cell phone to call the police.

Rory waved his hand and said, "No, Malina is all right."

Charlotte rubbed her eyes. She could have sworn she saw a haze in the air like heat emanating off a desert road. "Why does everyone keep saying I'm a human, like this is some kind of surprise?"

"Human?" Raibeart chuckled. "Of course ya are human. It's not like ya are a wolpertinger."

"A wolper—what?" Charlotte frowned.

"Wolpertinger," Raibeart said.

"All right, so I'm not a wolpertinger. But why does everyone have to point out that I'm human like I could be anything other than—"

"Of course you're not a wolpertinger," Raibeart interrupted. "They're Bavarian, and ya look to have a little bit of the Scots in ya, eh, red?"

"Raibeart!" Euann scolded. "Charlotte, don't answer that. The joke does not end appropriately."

"What are you two going on about?" Charlotte pressed her fingers against her temples. Wolpertingers and Bavaria?

Raibeart snickered. "Ya are no fun, lad. When she said no, she was not Scots, I was only going to ask if she wanted a little bit of Scot in her—"

"Hey!" Euann cut off his uncle. He shook his head in warning. "Stop talking. Not appropriate."

"But—"

"No," Euann stated.

"Sorry, Raibeart, I like my Scots big, not little," Charlotte quipped. At Euann's surprised look, she said, "Oh, please, I used to work in a bar. I've heard versions of that come-on line more times than I can count."

Raibeart started laughing and slapped his knee. "I knew I liked this one. Feisty, isn't she?"

"Would someone please tell me what is going on?" Charlotte eyed both men. She placed her hands on her hips. "Was that Dar guy a wolpertinger? And what exactly *is* a wolpertinger?"

"They are small creatures with the body of a rabbit, fangs, wings, and webbed feet like ducks," Niall stated, striding back into the room. "And they're not real. They were a hoax, like the American jackalope."

The sound of his voice caused her to stiffen and she turned to face him.

"Not true, you've only never seen one because you're not a young and beautiful woman." Raibeart appeared next to Charlotte and took her hand in his. "But ya are beautiful. What do ya say, my dear, shall we jump on the family jet and head over to Bavaria for an extended holiday? Together we can hunt the forest for wolpertingers, camp out under the stars, snuggle—"

"Oddly, that's the least strange thing I've heard all night," Charlotte said. Raibeart grinned and wagged his eyebrows as he moved closer to her.

"Where is Malina?" Euann asked.

"Raibeart, you're coming with me. Charlotte, you're staying here with Rory and Euann. They will protect ya." Niall motioned his hand like everyone would just unquestioningly follow his order.

"What?" Charlotte shook her head. "No. It's late. I'm going home. Alone. To sleep on my couch."

"Charlotte, ya should—" Niall stepped closer.

"Just stop," she ordered. "I'm not yours to command. Whatever weird shit you have happening here, I don't think I want to know about it. I just want..."

Her words trailed off as the smell of his cologne stirred a deep memory. She frowned, touching the center of her head. The tingling sensation that had given her clarity when Dar touched her intensified. A memory of a dark night began to take shape but was interrupted when Rory spoke.

"What's wrong with her?" Rory asked. "Did Dar give her too much, um, ah...?"

"Too much what?" Charlotte eyed the man, willing him to finish his sentence.

Rory looked at Niall for help. When no one answered, Rory finally said, "Bad luck." Niall made a sound of annoyance, to which Rory asked, "What? Do ya have a better answer? We all know what you're going to do to her after all this."

"We don't have time for this," Niall said. "Euann, watch over her."

"Yes." Euann nodded.

"Hey!" Charlotte grabbed Niall's arm.

A rush of energy exploded up her hand and arm. She gasped as her vision whitened. Color faded until everything looked like a black-and-white television show with bad reception, and sound became scratched like it played on an old record player.

"They're a cult," her recorded voice said. *"They're going to sacrifice us."*

Charlotte gasped again as something unlocked inside of her. Images rushed forward—of being kidnapped by two psychopaths and locked in a basement. Her jeans were stained from where she'd knelt in mud and her T-shirt was ripped along the seam. Someone had constructed metal bars like a prison cell.

How could she forget such a thing happening?

A hand touched her arm and she screamed, swinging a fist without even thinking. It made contact with skin. On impact, the memories stopped. She blinked to find Niall holding his face and stumbling away from her.

"Ha! Did ya see that?" Rory exclaimed. "She hit him!"

Rory and Euann started laughing uncontrollably. Charlotte glanced around in confusion. Her knuckles throbbed.

Raibeart slid an arm around her shoulders. "That's my girl!"

"Malina needs us," Niall muttered. "Raibeart come."

"Excuse me, lass," Raibeart lifted her hand and lightly kissed her sore knuckles, "but I have to go save the world now."

"Niall, I'm..." She started to apologize, but her mind was a swirl of memories, filling the present with a confusing rush of nonsense.

"I would take it all back if I could. I would rewind time if it would fix the future."

"Were you there?" Charlotte demanded, hearing the echo of his voice inside the memory of being kidnapped. She stared at Niall.

"Where?" he asked.

"The basement," she insisted. "I remember—"

Niall held up his hand. "I do not have time to discuss this with ya, Charlotte. Euann, take her to Cait. See if anything can be done about the seizures she mentioned."

Chapter Four

Just another day in the life of a warlock.

Niall held the broken demon blade in his hand and eyed the bubbling puddle of demon blood ruining the Georgian mansion's marble floor. The dining room was spacious, even with the shards of broken tables and chairs cluttering the floor. The abandoned junk pile of a goblin nest didn't exactly create the welcoming feel his family normally tried for. The house around them was trashed. There were cracks in the marble, stains on the walls, fractures in the wide-tread staircase, and splintered rails along the oak banister. Many of the furnishings were also in bad shape.

It had been a long time since a supernatural

attack of this magnitude and seriousness had taken place inside the family home. Euann was meticulous about security, placing protection spells around all the properties. It had taken some extremely bad luck to penetrate their barriers. In the end, the mansion was in shambles, the townsfolk were becoming too curious about magick, and Malina and Dar were back together. So all this fighting had been for nothing.

Niall should have felt exhilarated. They'd battled malevolent forces and won. They sent a demon back to hell, they rid the mansion of two very evil entities that looked like the spirits of two innocent girls, and they exorcised a heck of a lot of ghosts.

He wasn't though. Very little exhilarated him anymore. All he felt was exhaustion.

"I'll buy you a new demon blade," Malina offered, though they both knew that wasn't a possibility. One simply did not buy a demon blade from the local demon fighter store.

"Or not," Dar inserted quickly, as he tried to joke, "no reason to arm my brother-in-law who hates me."

Niall arched a brow. He didn't *hate* Dar, but he

did have a strong dislike for the fact his sister was reuniting with a demon. Life was dangerous enough without inviting it to join the family. And of course, now that Malina and her husband were reconciling, Niall was left looking like the asshole who'd tried to exorcise him.

"He doesn't hate you," Malina countered, clearly not realizing her brother could hear her. "Well, okay, he might, but he will come around."

"Do ya know how hard it is to find demon steel?" Niall stopped their conversation before it became too lovey-dovey. He waved the broken hilt in the air.

"Be happy it went to save the family." Malina sighed as she made a point of examining the house. "Ma and da are going to be so pissed when they get back. That's what you should be worried about. Not an old weapon."

Niall dropped the broken hilt. His sister had no idea how many times that knife had saved his life, had saved all of their lives. While she materialized designer clothes and ran off to marry demons who thought they were lost members of the rat pack, he was off fighting supernatural bad guys at the behest of the elders.

For the good of the clan.

To save the world.

To atone for his past transgressions.

Niall should have been happy the demon and the evil ghost children were back in hell, but he wasn't. Tomorrow there would only be another demon, or banshee, or goblin, or curse, or whatever. It never stopped. In centuries, it had never stopped.

Small talk had never been his strong suit, so he quickly ended the conversation with his sister and walked out the front door. The long drive coming up the hill was the only road access in or out. Currently, cars had created a traffic jam as the locals had come to check out some unfortunate light displays during the battle. Rory and Euann would be covering up the battle with some lame excuse about power surges and old wiring. People would believe it because it was rational.

Niall avoided the people near the driveway and made his way around the side of the house. There were a few outbuildings on the property, including an old coach house from the late eighteen hundreds. His brothers planned to turn the coach house into a garage. He would have used the exterior to hide a reinforced iron bunker with a weapons cache inside. It never hurt to be prepared when danger came. However, his brothers had outvoted him on that one and the garage won.

The mansion overlooked the small town in the valley below. A stretch of forest reached out from the back, creating privacy through nature. Because of their incredibly long lifespans, the family liked to move every couple of decades to prevent people from becoming suspicious. They'd been all over America throughout the years, Niall more so than the others.

If he were forced to choose, he'd have said this Wisconsin estate was one of his favorites. It had more nature than the New York penthouses, and less humidity than the Southern homes. Including the forest and a stream, the estate had around eighty acres. Six acres were the gardens in the back. He especially enjoyed the many walking paths that wound through the area. His brother Iain and Iain's new wife, Jane, had been tending the gardens and they were quite beautiful.

As Niall moved through the moonlight, he noticed new cracks in the foundation. A few spells would fix that right up, as well as repair all the damage done to the inside by the supernatural infestation they'd recently exorcised.

He did not want to think about where he was

going, even as he knew where his footsteps would lead. There was comfort in the quiet.

A foul smell wafted on the breeze and he grimaced. There was only one thing that smelled that bad. Apparently, they had not taken care of the goblin part of their problems. The little pest would have made a rotten den somewhere in the backyard but he was too tired to hunt it down right now.

He felt his body pull the magick from the trees as he moved down a shadowed path. Nature acted like a natural fuel. Power had to come from some-where, and although sexual pleasures could give a blast of energy, it tended to leave as fast as it came. Nature was a steady source, and being surrounded by so many trees meant they could borrow a little from the forest as a whole instead of killing a single tree. There had been times they'd almost killed off an entire forest while combating a formidable adversary. Though lately that didn't appear to be an issue since Jane's unique heritage made her like a battery supercharger for warlock power. And her single touch could repair damage to any plant.

The power running beneath the ground in Green Vallis's ley lines was incredible. It made sense that their magick had been drawn here and three of his siblings had found love. Well, it made sense for two of them.

Jane's addition to the family, he understood. Iain was in charge of replenishing nature, and Jane did that in abundance. Lydia's marriage to Erik, he understood. She was his natural *inthrall*, able to absorb her husband's power as her own. They had a deep connection that could not be broken. But Malina and a demon? That one was beyond him. The only thing he saw was his sister upsetting the order of things by creating her usual chaos with bad decisions.

Niall was not foolish enough to think he was destined for a mate. With his past, he wasn't exactly worthy of true love. He accepted that. The things he'd done were necessary. He kept the world safe and his family protected. But a person couldn't fight evil without getting dirty.

He touched his bruised eye. It was tender, but nothing he couldn't handle. He was baffled as to what had set Charlotte off and caused her to take a swing at him, but it was no more than he deserved.

The wind whistled through the tree limbs, singing an eerie song. He automatically looked to the sky, his warlock senses on alert. A twig snapped and he turned sharply toward the noise.

"I thought I'd find ya out here." Aunt Cait appeared from the shadows to block his path. She looked prim and proper in her skirt and silk blouse. Pearls hung from her ears and neck like a badge of feminine pride, and her heels did not belong on the rocky path. "There is nothing to be gained by staring at statues."

"I'm not going to the statue," he lied. "It has been a long night in a series of long nights. I am refueling my magick."

"Ya were going to the statue to dwell on the past," she scoffed. "Ya forget, laddie, I helped to raise ya. I can read ya like a book."

"Is there something ya need, Cait? I thought ya were looking after Charlotte." Niall was not in the mood for family drama.

"There is something unwell in that one," Cait said.

"Of course there is. I was told to erase her memories," Niall answered, his tone heavy. "If ya would have let me force her out of town when I asked, none of this would be happening."

"We can't leave her unsupervised," Cait warned him. Her voice sounded the same as it had when she'd scolded him as a young boy.

"Oh, aye, 'cause we're all doing such a splendid

job of protecting her—Euann and Rory petrified the poor girl; Erik and Malina had a magick fight in front of her before Erik shifted into cat form and called upon a tornado to attack her inside Lydia's house; she was forced by enchanted townsfolk to drink a potion and suck the power out of Iain, which left her partially insane—and that was just within our first months of being here. Shall I go on?"

"Don't take that tone with me," Cait warned. "Erik was under a love spell and couldn't help his actions. We saved Charlotte from those townsfolk and pulled the magick out of her. Don't forget, they nearly killed Iain. And a petrifying spell, really? They were all drinking, and it was my understanding she woke up with a hangover and didn't recall a thing. Ya act like we don't care about the poor girl. We have been doing all we can to keep her from falling over the edge into the dark place."

Niall did not need to be reminded of any of that. He knew the memories he'd taken from her, saw the things she'd been through, felt them as she'd felt them. All he wanted was to run from what he felt when he was near Charlotte, but his family kept shoving him back in her direction.

"Run for ya lives!" Raibeart burst from the

trees, barreling naked down the path with his hands in the air. He had a tiny claw mark on his backside. "*Gremains* stole my knickers."

Niall stiffened, and watched to see if any small creatures chased his uncle. After several moments, he lowered his guard. "I'm not chasing after—"

A small, knobby creature squealed and leapt out of the darkness. Niall stepped in front of Cait to protect her. The gremlin-like creature wore a pair of bright pink bikini briefs around his neck like a scarf. He gurgled some threat as he darted around Cait and Niall and continued after Raibeart.

"Please don't make me chase after my uncle's rogue underwear," Niall said.

Cait chuckled and patted his shoulder. "Ah, leave them. It's good that Raibeart made a friend. We have bigger things to worry about."

"Why are ya here, Cait?" Niall listened for the sound of more *gremains* in the forest. "I've done my duty. The mansion is safe. Malina has made her choice. There is nothing left for me tonight."

"Charlotte," Cait stated. "She has questions."

"Then answer her," Niall said. "I'm the last person she wants to see."

"She heard more than she should have tonight," Cait insisted.

Niall felt the anger rising inside of him, but he held it down. "I'm not going to take more from her. She's having seizures. We've already done too much."

"We didn't have a choice. After she absorbed Iain's magick, she would have gone insane if we had not taken action. The risk of exposure is too great. If she realizes that she..." His aunt closed her eyes. "I'm trying to fix it, but if any of the others realize what remains in her..."

Niall placed a hand on her shoulder. "I will take care of it. Where is she?"

Cait averted her gaze. "Your apartment."

Niall leaned over to make her face him. "What happened? Why did ya leave her alone?"

Cait made a weak noise. "She was asking a lot of questions, so I might have cast a small petrifying spell."

Niall loved his family, but there were times he wanted to cast a bubble spell over them to keep them locked up and out of mischief.

"And ya want me to take care of it?" It wasn't really a question as he already knew the answer. Of course they wanted him to deal with it. The whistling wind picked back up.

"Listen to that. Something is not happy," Cait mused, looking up at the trees.

"Aye, it didn't want to see Raibeart's naked arse any more than I did," Niall muttered.

"That sounds like a wraith. It was probably drawn to the house with the other ghosts when Malina's luck demon found a way through our protection spells." Cait fingered her pearl necklace. "We need to take care of it."

His aunt might have said "we" but Niall knew where the responsibility would land. He closed his eyes and took a deep breath. In no particular order: clear out stinky goblin den, make sure no ghosts were still hiding in the mansion, hunt *gremains* before they took apart the whole town brick by brick, track down a demon blade, exorcise a wraith, ensure he didn't have to kill Malina's husband a second time, and fix Charlotte's apartment because he'd apparently been failing as a landlord.

Damn Dar and his dose of bad luck.

Then there was Charlotte herself. She didn't belong on his list of chores as she wasn't simply a chore. He needed to protect her.

"There is something different about Charlotte tonight," Cait said, getting the conversation back on track. "I have done all I can for her, but Euann said the luck demon touched her. If it was bad luck, I'm guessing she'd be dead by now. But I cannot predict what his brand of good luck will do to the spells we've been casting to help her."

Niall thought about the statue. His guilt would not be taking him there this night.

Chapter Five

Niall looked at the woman frozen in mid-action on his couch. Charlotte wore a pair of jeans and a long sweater, and he was glad to see her out of the wet clothes from earlier. By the way her arm was braced, it appeared she had been trying to get up. Whereas he understood Cait probably didn't have a choice, he hated that magick was used on Charlotte yet again.

He lifted his hand, pushing the apartment door shut behind him without touching it. Charlotte couldn't move, not even her eyes, and he knew anything he said or did would not register. To her, she would be locked in a dream. He listened to the door lock latch behind him before moving toward her.

She was beautiful as if carved from a Renaissance master's chisel. There was a wildness in her gaze that haunted him because he knew he was partly responsible for it. In trying to save her, he had broken her. Her curls wound around her head, frozen like the snake hair of Medusa. It was a fitting comparison, not that she was a monster or hideous to behold, but because like the ancient gorgon, she could turn him to stone with just one look. When Charlotte gazed upon him, spoke to him, he became unable to respond.

Niall took a seat next to her, and leaned his head back against the couch. "I am sorry, Charlotte, that we find ourselves yet again in a magickal circumstance. Ya don't deserve any of this."

She couldn't hear him.

"I love my family, but ya won't believe the mess they made this time." For a moment, he let himself imagine she sat next to him willingly, and that this was normal. "Maybe I should take ya away from here? We could get on my bike and ride and..."

What was he doing? This wasn't a date. Charlotte didn't even like him. He touched his sore cheek where she'd punched him.

After several long moments sitting in silence,

he finally lifted his head to look at her. He placed his hand on her back, between her shoulder blades. The skin had lost all pliability. He patted her a few times, wishing she could feel the comfort somehow in her dreams.

He let his hand fall away from her and leaned forward, bracing his arms on his knees. He let the memories he carried flow through him as a reminder as to why he'd taken them. He made himself feel the fear she had in being locked in a basement prison, the feeling of Iain's magick entering her by force and those eternal seconds when death had lingered inside of her.

"There is so much work to be done, and all I want to do is sleep," he whispered. "Sometimes I think about stopping and making someone else deal with the dangers of the world, but I can't abandon my family or my duty."

The echoes of screams lingered inside him. Charlotte had been terrified when she watched Erik shift into a half panther, half man. He could just imagine how she'd react seeing his wolf. Niall stared at the tip of his forefinger, letting hair grow over the digit as a nail shifted into a sharp claw. He shook his hand, making it return to normal.

Niall knew what his duty was. He was to protect the MacGregor clan at all cost. He was to fight evil in all forms. Magick needed to be hidden and contained. The easiest thing would have been to let Charlotte fall into her insanity and be dismissed as another sad story in the history of mental health.

He couldn't do it.

Niall paced the length of his living room. The apartment didn't feel like a home. It felt like just another room, a place to store his weapons if he ever decided to unpack them from his motorcycle.

"I would take it all back if I could," he told her, not for the first time. The only time he could manage to get words out around her was when she couldn't hear them. Niall found himself kneeling before her. He gazed at her face. "I would rewind time if I thought it would help fix your future."

As badly as he wanted her to speak to him, he was just as glad that she couldn't hear his words. There was nothing to be gained by her learning the truth—any of the truths. Remembering the pain and fear of the past would not help her. Discovering the knowledge he kept buried would not cure her.

"I would let ya see the truth if that meant ya

would look at me once the way I see ya every day." The feelings he suppressed whenever she was around tried to fill him. He looked around the apartment, trying to reassure himself that no one would ever discover the truth of what he was about to say. The words barely left him in a whisper. "I love ya, Charlotte."

And that was the truth he tried so hard to hide from everyone. He loved her from that very first moment. It had shot through him like a bullet, and like a bullet the knowledge left a giant hole inside him. He promised himself he would not say the words out loud again even if she couldn't hear them. His feelings were a burden she did not need. He touched his bruised eye. He saw the way she looked at him.

Niall's dreams were filled with her. They may always be filled with her, but she deserved more than a man who chased demons for a living. He hated to admit it, but she deserved a man like his brother Euann.

There wasn't much he could do for her in her current state but wait. Niall lifted her into his arms and carried her to his bed. As the spell wore off, she'd be able to relax. He arranged her the best he could and covered her with a blanket.

"I promise ya, Charlotte, I will find a way to help ya." He kept his voice a whisper, even as he knew no one else was in the apartment to hear. "And I will keep my feelings to myself. They will never be your burden to deal with."

Chapter Six

Charlotte couldn't move, not that she wanted to. All around her, black-and-white images played like virtual reality. Vertigo came and went as she clung to moments when the ground was solid and did not slide from under her.

People she knew from town appeared in front of her, rudely close, flashing across her vision. Their voices did not match the movements of their mouths. The metal tin of a star hung in front of the country drive. Sheriff Johnson's house had such a star in front of it. Firelight danced over it.

She began to shake, knowing instinctively that nothing good was going to come from this. Hands gripped her and she found Lydia holding on to her. Shadows cast all around in the light, long and distorted as townsfolk danced. There was a young girl from town with flaxen ringlets, and her mother. Mrs. Callister, the busybody who snooped into everyone's business, passed near Mr. Baker from the post office and Mr. Wirth, their third-grade teacher. Chef Alana wore an apron as if she'd just been called out of her kitchen. Charlotte loved Alana's fettuccini with basil and tomato.

The young girl fetched an ornate goblet from the ground. A strange chanting began amongst the townsfolk. This had to be a dream. What else could it be? She tried to wake up. She scratched her arm, unable to feel.

A dark shadow cut through the light. Charlotte heard a scream echoing around them, reverberating inside her. The dark spirit circled the fire and was joined by another.

The young girl brought the goblet to her. A voice from behind ordered, "Drink it."

Time became meaningless. Charlotte found the cup in her hands. She saw liquid flying from her lips, the blood-red poison standing out against the colorless world. The child screamed as droplets hit her dress, and she ran to her mother. Charlotte's mouth was again open as she swallowed mouthfuls. It was a taste that could not easily be forgotten.

The cup disappeared, and she was on her back, looking up at the night sky. Her limbs jerked and seized as the insane energy flowed into her and out of her.

"I would take it all back if I could," a familiar voice whispered against her cheek, different from the others. "I would rewind time if it would fix the future. I would let ya see the truth."

The firelight faded onto gray walls, taking the voices with it. She wanted to run, but her body did not obey. She blinked, her lids feeling heavy. The dark shadows swam over the walls, calling to a place deep within her brain. These were not like the ghosts she'd seen. Gramma Annabelle's spirit was soft and light, and smelled of lilies.

"I remember you," she tried to say to the shadows, though she wasn't sure her lips actually moved, or her voice had left her. "I remember you are a *lidérc*. You came to me. No, we were brought to you. No, you needed us for something...?"

Charlotte held on to all the pieces she could, clinging to the fragments as she struggled to arrange them into their rightful places. The shadows faded and were replaced by the softness of early morning light. The rumble of cars moved over the street. It was the sounds of her apartment, but her walls were not gray and her bed was not dry. She heard the rhythmic tapping of a hammer somewhere beyond the room.

Her limbs wouldn't move, but she ignored them as she tried to hold on to the images she'd seen. There were gaps in her memory, but the timeline began to fill in. She'd been locked in a basement with Lydia. They'd been taken to Sheriff Johnson's lawn, where there had been bonfires. That didn't seem like a real memory. Sheriff Johnson waved at her every time she saw him. He hardly seemed the type to have scary bonfires on his lawn. Yet, she was as sure of it as she was her memory of stringing Buck Mitchell to the flagpole.

They'd wanted her to drink something. The awful taste of the poison had flooded her mouth and nearly killed her. Then her body had been filled with energy and pain. Had she been electrocuted? Is that why her memories stopped? Lightning? Downed power line? Jumper cables? None of those answers seemed like the right one.

As excited as she was to remember something, anything, from her lost time, she was just as terrified to see what lay hidden in there. Had the entire town gone insane and tried to sacrifice her and her best friend? She'd heard people talking about some kind of bad mushroom incident at a potluck dinner. Had she ingested poisonous mushrooms and hallucinated?

A familiar scent caused her to turn her head toward the pillow. It both irritated and excited her at once. She knew that smell. Niall?

A blue flash of light spread over the room and she gasped as her limbs seemed to let loose. She flailed, turning in confusion as she tangled in the bedding. Her mind processed her surroundings slowly. She was in a strange bed, but fully dressed in a sweater and blue jeans. The room lacked in decoration, aside from the bed and a small table with an open duffel bag. Clothes poked out of the top as if someone had dug through it.

I would take it all back if I could. I would rewind time if it would fix the future. I would let ya see the truth.

Niall.

Charlotte's motions became deliberate as she freed herself from the covers. Everything kept coming back to him. He was always there in the background, watching her. He owned her building. He whispered in her returning memories. Now she was in his bed.

"Niall?" she called before leaving the bedroom.

The apartment appeared empty. She caught her reflection as she passed the bathroom door. Seeing the mess of her hair, she instantly walked toward the mirror. The wildness of her appearance took her by surprise as if she hadn't looked at herself in the mirror in a while. Her red hair was much brighter than normal, and the fact that it looked like she hadn't bothered with a brush only added to the cavewoman effect. Her misbuttoned shirt forced her collar to fall strangely to the side.

Charlotte did her best to right her appearance, rebuttoning the shirt and untangling the elastic band from her hair. She tried to find a brush but aside from a razor, toothbrush, and a few odds and ends, the drawers were empty. However, she did notice a bottle of the Love Potions body wash she and Lydia made in his shower.

"I brought ya lunch."

Charlotte gasped at the sound of Niall's voice and slammed a drawer shut as she whipped around in the bathroom to face him. She hadn't heard him come up behind her. "I wasn't, I was…"

His eyes narrowed as he studied her. "Is this a seizure?"

"No." She placed her hands on her hips. He wore a faded T-shirt and distressed jeans. She could barely count the times he hadn't been in a kilt. The bruise by his eyes caused her to flex her hand unconsciously. "I'm saying, I wasn't snooping. I was looking for a brush for my hair."

"Why would I have a brush for your hair?" he asked.

"Why would I be in your bed?" she countered. That's not what she'd meant. It was too late to retract her words as their implications unraveled, her mind only too happy to supply her with many varied answers to that question. There was only one way out of the bathroom and he was blocking it. Flustered, she tried to rephrase. "I mean, why would you have me in your bed? Or rather, why am I in your..."

Charlotte held up her hands and shook her head. She averted her eyes and pushed forward, forcing him to back away as she made her way into the living room. Several food containers were on the table from various places in town—fast food burgers, Chinese takeout, a couple of pizza boxes, tacos, and boxes labeled Perfection Restaurant.

"Is this what you eat for breakfast?" Charlotte frowned.

"It's lunch." Niall pointed at a drink carrier. "Tea, coffee, soda, lemonade?"

"Uh, tea." Charlotte glanced out the window. She'd assumed it was morning, but it could have been later in the day. Had she really slept that long?

He handed the iced tea to her and gestured at the pizzas. "Super cheese or beef with mushrooms."

Charlotte arched a brow and didn't speak.

He continued around the strange buffet. "Lo mien noodles, sesame ginger chicken, steak tacos, chicken quesadilla, cheeseburger with tater tots, chicken strips and fries, fettuccini with basil and tomato, or chicken Parmesan?"

"Who's coming to lunch?" Charlotte ignored the fact that he'd somehow shown up with all of her favorites from around town.

He frowned and shook his head. "Just us. I did not know what ya would want. As my family constantly points out, I do not have a home suited to guests. There is no food in the fridge."

If this had been anyone else, she would have thought the gesture sweet, but this was Niall—grumpy, moody, disapproving, pain-in-the-ass Niall.

Even though she was hungry, she didn't move to take the food. She set the tea down on the table and crossed her arms over her stomach. "Did something happen? I seem to remember talking to your Aunt Cait, standing up to leave, and then...nothing."

"Ya slept in my bed," he said, as if that was enough of an answer.

Seeing a discarded bathrobe beside the table, she remembered what Raibeart had said about her. "I'm not crazy."

He continued to look at her with his unreadable expression. She wondered what went on inside his mind. What had happened to him to make him like this? The rest of his family was fun-loving and chaotic. Niall was so controlled to the point he appeared rigid, and his rare smiles were like sighting an endangered animal in the wild.

"No. I would not say ya are crazy." The words were slow in coming as if he wasn't sure she was looking for an answer.

"The man who was here last night," she began.

"Darragh Lahey," Niall supplied. "Dar."

"Did he do something to Malina? I wanted to check on her last night, but I don't remember leaving the apartment. Instead, I woke up in your bed." She really needed to stop pointing out she'd been in his bed. Each time she said it, the fact sounded more intimate than it had a right to be. She'd probably blacked out again and they hadn't known what to do with her.

"It was a family matter. Malina is unharmed. Dar is her husband. They were having an argument, but it is settled now." Niall gave a meaningful look at the food. Charlotte ignored the gesture.

"I'm not crazy," she stated.

"Ya said that already," he reminded her.

"There is something different about your family." She ignored his curt response.

"Aye. We're Scottish." Niall's tone was dry, and it took her a moment to realize he might be attempting to make a joke. Then again, she wasn't sure.

"No, not that."

"We wear kilts."

"No."

"We're rich."

"You know what I mean." She braced her hand on the back of a dining chair in irritation.

"I don't." His expression gave nothing away and she had to resist the temptation to blacken his other eye. Violence was never the answer, but there was something about him that stirred her blood and made her want to scream.

"You have secrets. And not just the mommy-had-an-affair, daddy-didn't-love-us, our-brother-has-warrants-in-five-states type of secrets."

"None of those things is true, and I find it offensive that ya would suggest it." Niall reached for a chair and pulled it away from the table. He looked at her expectantly. "Ya should eat."

"You really are going to make me say it, aren't you?" Charlotte took a deep breath. She knew what her words would sound like before she said them. "You all have superpowers, or special gifts, or something not quite normal going on."

"Aye, my ma says we're all special little snowflakes," he drawled sarcastically. "Now, please, eat something."

"Dammit, Niall," she yelled, tossing her hands in desperation. "Help me out here, because if what I know to be true *isn't* true, then I *am* insane and there's no hope that I can get better!"

"What makes ya think we have superpowers?"

At least he wasn't laughing as he asked the question. "Nothing has been right since your family came to town."

"That is hardly evidence of—"

"When Dar touched me, I felt as if he gave me Malina's energy. I haven't felt this clearheaded in a long while. I'm remembering things...like being held captive in a basement, and these floating blue balls of light streaming over Lydia's lawn. I remember people that I know and talk to every day handing me poison in a goblet. I remember..." Charlotte began to shake as more thoughts rushed in. "Erik's face changed. Erik and Malina were throwing light from their hands at each other. Erik made the weather attack Lydia's house."

"That's impossible," Niall said.

Charlotte took a deep breath. Saying the words out loud had made her sound insane.

"There is no way ya can remember any of that. Who told ya?" Niall's expression changed by small degrees until his eyes felt like they pierced her with their intensity. Their color shifted from a hard brown that chilled her to a smoldering hazel that warmed every part of her.

"I'm really not crazy," she answered in surprise. "It's true. All of it."

Niall nodded.

"Why are you in the memories? Did you kidnap me?" She took several steps back to consider what she had just said. The idea sent a shiver up her spine. Was that why she was always nervous around him?

"You're talking about separate events. Erik was entranced by a prank my sister tried on him, and they argued by throwing magick at each other. Then ya witnessed him shifting into panther form on Lydia's lawn and calling upon the weather in his desperation to get to her."

"But she married Erik." Startled by what she heard, Charlotte still tried to reason what he was telling her. At this time, there wasn't an abundance of explanations for what was going on, so she gave the only person forthcoming his chance to explain. "And what about the kidnapping?"

"That was not my family's doing. Ya were taken by a couple of men who were possessed by a sort of psychic vampire. The *lidérc* like to latch on to weaknesses they find in people's psyche and then crawl around inside their minds to control them. My family is naturally immune to such attacks, but the *lidérc* crave the power we have, so they entranced the townspeople to help them get it. They made ya an *inthrall* so they could use ya to suck the magick from my brother Iain. We managed to stop them, but it left Iain in a coma and my ma had to work an enchantment spell to preserve him until he was well enough to wake up."

"What did it do to *me*? Was I in a coma? Is that why I can't remember?" Charlotte rubbed her arms, feeling cold. Her eyes strayed to the window, but didn't see much beyond the top of a building down the block.

"It nearly killed ya. The family called me in both after Erik scared ya and after the kidnapping, to ensure ya didn't remember the events. I erased your memory. You'll have to take me at my word when I say I did ya a favor."

Realization slowly dawned on her. Niall was responsible for her lost memories. She also knew that she'd lost time more than twice.

"How are ya?" he asked carefully, not taking his eyes off her.

"Are you kidding me?" Charlotte placed her hands on her hips. "Do you know what I've been through? Do you know how many medical bills I have run up trying to figure out what's wrong with my head? Not to mention the nightmares, and worry, and..." She gasped. "Oh, god, and you let Lydia marry Erik! She was there, too, wasn't she? You took our memories and then let—"

Niall's eyes shifted away from her.

"What?"

"Lydia has her memories," he said. "During the process, she was able to filter Erik's magick back to him and stop the transfer of energy. She came out of it unharmed. Since she is a natural *inthrall* to Erik, there was no need to help her the way I did ya."

"Help," she repeated. At first, she was angry that he dared to pretend what he did had helped her. Then, a deeper truth became apparent. If Lydia remembered everything, then she had known the answers all along. "You think taking my memories helped me?"

"There is more at stake than ya can understand —" Niall said.

"Stop." Charlotte held up her hand to keep him from talking. She couldn't hear any more. Slowly, she turned and walked toward his door. Then, stopping, she turned and grabbed the bag with the Italian takeout from the table and said, "I'm taking this."

"Char—"

"Don't follow me," she ordered.

Chapter Seven

"When I like died, I like told my husband to drop me somewhere beautiful. I meant a fountain in the middle of a shopping complex or something. But he was like an idiot and he found a pretty creek and scattered me into it." The ghost looked as if she'd died in the '80s during an unfortunate hair crimping accident, and spoke with the annoying ditziness of a Valley girl. The end of each sentence rose in pitch like she was asking a question, even when she wasn't.

Charlotte took a deep breath, willing the spirit to stop talking. She tried concentrating on what she'd discovered about her missing memories, and the dead woman wouldn't give her a moment's peace.

Some apparitions flashed in and out of view suddenly, like they'd seen one too many jump-scares in horror movies, and liked to startle those who could see them. Others, like the annoyance chattering away beside her, floated as if stirred by an invisible breeze.

Sheriff Johnson's squad car drove past. The man lifted his hand out of the driver's side window in greeting. Charlotte's heart quickened as thoughts of what happened on the sheriff's lawn surged forward. She barely managed a weak smile in return, and walked faster.

Amber didn't pay attention to their surroundings as the whine of her voice became a steady buzz. "Little did I know Wisconsin is where I would be stuck for eternity. If I did, I would have been a little more specific in my locations."

Charlotte glanced behind her at downtown. She wasn't sure her small town deserved the disdain in Amber's diatribe. The red brick streets weren't too busy. The weather was mild, not that the ghost would have been able to tell. People waved at each other, talked about football and the new local celebrities, the MacGregors. The streets were clean, the children —*mostly*—behaved, and neighbors helped neighbors.

Charlotte shivered, again thinking of the bonfire. Neighbors had been there, helping her to drink from a goblet of poison. A couple of cars moved past. Town gossip, Mrs. Callister, drove slower than the speed limit, much to the obvious dismay of the family of four stuck behind her. She had a pencil stuck behind her ear, always ready to jot down anything she considered newsworthy. The old woman's eyes met Charlotte's in disapproval. That was nothing new, but Charlotte also remembered Callister's face highlighted by fire and her lips moving as if to chant.

Amber kept babbling. "You would have thought he had the sense to take me to California. There is like no shopping here and nature is grotty to the max. I saw a dog relieving himself in the woods and the owner just left it."

Charlotte paused on her way up the hill toward Lydia's house. "Hey, Amber, you should like go find the light or something." Charlotte mocked the spirit's Valley girl accent.

"Like, for sure," Amber agreed. "So how long have you been dead?"

How long had it been since Amber started talking to her?

"About twenty minutes," Charlotte answered, again quickening her pace.

"Bummer. We should definitely—" Amber's words abruptly stopped and she was gone.

Charlotte took a deep breath. Ghosts were a relatively new development in her life, and they didn't find her too often. The only one she saw consistently was Lydia's Gramma Annabelle. Since she'd always believed in the possibility of ghosts, she had an easier time than most accepting spirits when they first appeared. However, something no one ever seemed to take into consideration was that, being formerly alive people, ghosts could be as annoying as they were in life. Take chatty Amber for example. She'd hardly paused in her twenty-minute ode to her own awesome.

Though Charlotte wasn't sure what happened to Amber's spirit, she could guess that the protective mojo Annabelle had put around the house during her life had blocked the ghost from following. As a green witch, Annabelle had been all about protective spells and potions, herbs and natural healing.

Charlotte didn't bother to knock as she pulled open the screen door and entered Lydia's kitchen. No one used the front door as the kitchen entry led out to the driveway and sidewalk to town. The old Victorian might be Lydia's home, but it was also Charlotte's place of work. The house had originally belonged to the estate on the hill, and had been built for the estate owner's mother-in-law. Later the house became servants' quarters before finally being purchased by Lydia's grandfather. Lydia inherited it when Gramma Annabelle died. The MacGregors now owned the mansion on the hill, and with Lydia's marriage to Erik MacGregor, it looked like the estate was once again made whole.

Charlotte nearly tripped on the handcart they used to haul packages down the hill to the post office. Irritated by the mishap, she grumbled as she sidestepped the trolley and put the food bags on the table. She had hoped the walk would calm her temper and give her some answers, but she was still shaking—her nerves were raw as ever, and her mind whirred worse than before.

The smell of lilies filled the air and she glanced around the familiar kitchen. The pink curtains were new, but still reminded Charlotte of Gramma Annabelle's old-fashioned décor. The cream-colored walls were the same as they always were. Lotion bottles were lined up on the countertops, ready to be filled. Love Potions' storefront was technically the living room off the kitchen, with a small entryway by the front door. Shelves filled the space, with overflow stored in a coat closet, cabinets, and about anywhere else they could shove a bottle of lotion. Locals seemed to enjoy the homey atmosphere and never complained about stopping in to pick up their orders. A stairwell led to three bedrooms and a bathroom. Lydia lived there with her husband now, but there had been many nights Charlotte crashed in a guest room.

The business had nearly tripled in sales over the last year. Euann had worked on redesigning the company website and now orders were pouring in. There had even been discussion of renting a building downtown and hiring a couple of part-time workers to handle the extra production.

Yes, Charlotte knew orders were a good thing, and she was happy that Lydia's business was taking off. But as the business grew, it lost the laid-back feel she loved. Like Charlotte's apartment, this house used to be a sanctuary. Now nothing made sense. Everything was changing.

"You might as well come out, I can smell the lilies," Charlotte said as she placed the food bags on the table. She retrieved a fork from the silverware drawer and sat down. As angry as she was, her stomach had been growling in protest and she couldn't resist Alana's fettuccini with basil and tomato.

Annabelle materialized wearing the green, sparkling ball gown she'd been buried in. Her transparent form wasn't as strong as it had been in the past, but she looked completely aware of her surroundings. When she moved, she glided more than walked.

"Hello, sweet dear," Annabelle said softly.

Charlotte shoved a forkful of pasta into her mouth.

"How are you?" the ghost insisted.

She shoved in another forkful and chewed.

"Oh, poo. You're mad."

At Annabelle's mild version of cussing, Charlotte arched a brow and looked directly at her.

"It was only once. Or twice. Not more than a dozen times." Annabelle smiled guiltily. "I swear I didn't hurt you. I just tried to hitch a ride so that I could carry spell bags of my hair and blood out into town. I really want to increase my haunting territory and Lydia won't do it for me. She thinks I'll cause trouble and start appearing to the wrong people."

Annabelle had been trying to possess her? Charlotte didn't say a word.

"You tell me you don't think that ol' goody two-shoes Mrs. Callister doesn't deserve a little friendly haunting. How many times did she publish nonsense about us in her little community news-letter?" Annabelle paused, as if expecting an answer.

"You jumped into my body?"

"You were sleeping," Annabelle said, as if that made it all right. "You didn't know? That's not why you're mad?"

Charlotte turned to her meal with renewed force. The more she found out truths, the more she wasn't sure she could take any more. What would be next? She'd be abducted by aliens and probed?

"So, you figured the other thing out, did you?" Annabelle became a little more corporeal as if she'd put more thought into manifesting herself. She crossed over to Charlotte and placed a hand on her arm to keep her from angrily filling her mouth another time. "Slow down or you'll choke."

Charlotte couldn't feel the touch, except for the extreme cold radiating from transparent fingers, and lifted her fork to take another bite. A shiver ran over her as she passed through the hand. When she swallowed, she grumbled, "Why? Don't you want company?"

Annabelle's body dissipated into a blurry gust of air as she blew against the to-go container on the table and slid it away from Charlotte's angry fork. Charlotte was already in mid-action and stabbed the table.

"Hey," Charlotte protested.

"I know you're upset, but there will be no more talk of dying on my watch." Annabelle fluttered back to stand in front of Charlotte. She gestured over her transparent body. "Death is no picnic. Sure, I look great all the time, and I've clearly lost weight, and I can still stick my nose in people's business, and floating through walls is fun, and—"

"Are you convincing me to join you or not to join you? I'm confused." Charlotte reached across the table for her food and pulled it back in front of her. This time when she ate, she was a little calmer about it.

"Your life isn't even half over," Annabelle said. "You have so much—"

"Everyone I know lied to me. They let me believe I was crazy, that I was blacking out and losing time. But it turns out the nightmares are true. Sheriff Johnson had a bonfire on his lawn and

I was the main event at the barbeque. Apparently, Lydia married a shifter cat man who is magical and throws balls of light as his sister."

"I know it's a lot to take in, but—"

Charlotte felt sorrow replacing the anger. "All that I can handle. I can take the entire world falling apart around me."

Lydia appeared in the doorway of the kitchen and smiled in surprise. "Char, hi, I didn't hear you come in."

Charlotte looked at Lydia, but continued speaking to Annabelle. "But what I can't deal with, Gramma, is my best friend lying to me."

"Wait, what?" Lydia gasped, looking at the spirit of her grandmother for help. "Charlotte...?"

Charlotte pointed at the chicken Parmesan container still in the food bag. "I brought you lunch, and I quit."

Lydia gasped again. Annabelle tried to speak but Charlotte didn't hear her. Unsure what she was doing, she stood up and walked out of the kitchen door.

"Wait, Charlotte!" Lydia called after her. "Come back! I can explain. I..."

Charlotte walked faster, fighting tears. For some reason, she found herself moving away from town into the woods. She didn't want to meet up with Niall, or Amber, or the townsfolk she'd called friends. She'd prayed to fill in the missing time, and now that she had answers, she wished she could forget again.

"Hey, can you see me yet?"

Charlotte automatically glanced at the woman's spirit standing by a tree. It was a reflex, and she instantly regretted it. The woman had long brown hair and wore a white gown. The details of the transparent figure were hard to distinguish, but it could have been a modest nightgown of sorts. The words were accented and soft, like an English lady. Perhaps the former lady of the estate, or a maid? Such a thing would not be unheard of.

"Oh, good, finally." The ghost drifted to walk alongside Charlotte. "Please, you have to tell me, where am I? Where is this place?"

She hoped answering would send the spirit away. "Green Vallis, Wisconsin, in the woods. You're dead. You should move on. There's nothing for you here."

"I don't know this Wisconsin," the ghost said. "Tell me, which way to Huntingdon?"

Charlotte frowned. With the accent, the ghost probably meant some place in England.

"My father has a farm near there. If you would but help me in the right direction, I am sure I can find my way home." The ghost lifted her hand in a rolling gesture that blurred in the air.

"You're a long way from England." Charlotte walked faster, ducking her head as she moved through the trees.

"The helpless act is not working, is it?" The ghost's voice changed from the confused whispers of a lost soul to irritation. "Shame. It's so much easier if you'd open yourself up and come with me willingly."

Charlotte stopped suddenly as the apparition appeared in front of her. The face had changed from the docile maiden to a frightening lady with sunken eyes and cheeks. The pupils of her eyes were completely white and her skin moved as if covered by tiny insects.

"No bother," the ghost stated nonchalantly. Her brown hair flew, enveloping her shoulders and then spiraling around her features, even in the still forest where there was neither wind nor breeze to speak of. "We'll do this the hard way."

Chapter Eight

Niall had followed Charlotte on foot, keeping his distance while watching her as she went up the hill toward Lydia's house. He'd wanted to make sure she was safe. Aside from a ghost he'd seen wandering around a few times, no one bothered her. It went against everything in him to tell her the truth, especially since he'd worked so hard to hide it. MacGregors had to keep their magick a secret from the rest of the world.

There had been something in her eyes when she'd looked at him. She'd appeared so lost. But more than that, she recalled memories that should not have been there. An erased memory was supposed to be gone forever. They didn't simply grow back.

At least she'd gone to Lydia. She'd be safe there.

He paused, thinking of going back to watch the house, just to be sure Charlotte stayed inside. But she was at work and would be there all day.

Reaching into his pocket, he pulled out his cell phone and continued through the trees on the path leading from Lydia's house to the MacGregor estate.

"Cait MacGregor," his aunt answered.

"Ya were right. Charlotte is different. She remembers," Niall said without bothering with a greeting.

"Remembers what?" Cait whispered.

"Almost everything. Enough to demand I fill in the blanks of her missing time," he admitted. "Dar's luck infusion clearly affected her."

"That's not enough to regrow memories," Cait said, "but with all the spells we've been casting to help her through this, and nearly dying from being bombarded with Iain's powers thanks to the *lidérc*... who knows what's happening inside that poor lass?"

Niall could still feel the fear he'd taken from Charlotte. At least that crazed look hadn't returned to her eyes along with the memories. That was something.

"Where are ya now?" Cait asked.

"I just left Erik and Lydia's and I'm on my way up to the estate. I followed Charlotte there. She should be fine with her friend."

"Good thing Erik was able to cast spells to cover up the *gremain* damage," Cait said. "That is one less piece of wreckage we need to explain."

"Da called early this morning and asked me to handle reports of a water sprite migration. I'm stopping by the mansion to pick up a few potion bottles and enchanted blades. Charlotte's not going to be happy, so I need ya to go to Lydia's and keep an eye on her. Petrify her until I get back if ya have to, but promise me there will be no more memory-erasing spells, or potions, or luck infusions until I can handle it."

"No, lad, ya stay where ya are. I'll send Murdoch to handle the sprites. We need ya to deal with Charlotte."

Niall stopped walking and looked at the ground. He took a deep breath. A deep part of him wanted to turn and go to Charlotte, eager to be near her. Another, deeper part, told him to refuse and run. He would rather battle a vampire, or fight a werewolf, or even clean out the goblin den smelling up the back gardens.

"Don't ask this of me," he whispered, dropping the phone away from his mouth.

"Niall?" Cait insisted. "Did ya hear me?"

"Aye," Niall answered. "I hear ya."

"Good. I'll do all I can, but that lass is a ticking bomb. Ya know what ya saw inside her. She can't have that kind of power."

"Cait, I hear ya," he said more forcefully. "I'll leave it to ya to explain to Da why I can't handle the sprites."

"Don't ya worry about your da. I'll tell him we need ya here, close to the family to deal with the aftermath of this estate mess. Your brothers can repair the home. Margareta and I will charm the town."

"Don't ya think there is enough magick floating around?" Niall turned to look back toward Lydia's house, hidden by trees. His eyes shifted as he focused his attention, but he could not see through trees. A familiar smell caught his attention, and he veered off the footpath into the underbrush.

"Female charm, not magick," Cait corrected.

"We women have a delicate way about us. Something men know little about."

"I beg to differ, Cait." Niall sniffed, following the trail. He braced the phone with his shoulder and let claws grow from his nail beds. He kept his tone even, not giving away any concerns. "We men know the dangers of female charms all too well." He bent under a low-hanging branch. "Why do ya think we're always obeying?"

"Good, then ya won't have any problem obeying this order. Wait, hold on..." Cait's words became muffled as she talked to someone else.

While she was distracted, Niall used the opportunity to run several paces, leaping over the brush to land silently in a small clearing. His uncle, Raibeart, slept naked on the ground using a fallen tree limb as a blanket. Thankfully, leaves covered his privates. Niall grimaced and retracted his claws.

"Handle Charlotte. Ya know what needs to be done. I need ya to be strong for the family, Niall," Cait continued as if she hadn't been interrupted. "The ghosts will wander off on their own eventually, but make sure that wraith doesn't cause any problems, and exterminate the goblin—"

"Eh, now, is that any way to talk about Uncle Raibeart?" Niall teased, purposefully misunderstanding what she meant by the goblin. Raibeart made a small noise in his sleep and moved his hand to cover something on his chest. Niall leaned to the side to better see.

"I'm glad ya think this is funny," she scolded.

Raibeart's hand moved as if petting something. "Fine, Cait, I'll do as ya ask, but answer me one important thing."

"Aye?"

The *gremain* with Raibeart's underwear around his neck lifted his head from Raibeart's chest before snuggling down and going back to sleep. "If Raibeart gets with that *gremain* chasing his naked arse through the forest last night, would that make it an elder, and would I have to take orders from—?"

Cait hung up without answering.

Niall chuckled and couldn't resist lifting his phone to take a picture of the couple before moving to wake him. He nudged Raibeart's leg with the toe of his boot. "Eh, rise and shine, buttercup."

Raibeart groaned and swatted at the boot. The movement caused the *gremain* to groan and jump up. The creature hissed at Niall before taking off into the woods. Niall didn't give chase.

"Raibeart, get up," he ordered. "Cait needs ya at the house. It's an emergency."

His uncle sat up and lifted his arms into a boxing stance. His eyes didn't open, as he said, "I'm on it."

"We're being attacked by giant chickens. A whole swarm of them," he said. "And they're being led by a wolpertinger. It's a mess. Feathers are everywhere. The chickens are winning. You're our last hope."

Raibeart opened one eye as if to test the light and scrambled to his feet, swaying slightly. "Never fear, *wulver*, I will save the family." He stumbled in the wrong direction.

"That way," Niall corrected, pointing toward the mansion.

Raibeart blinked, looked around, then nodded. He marched naked through the woods.

Niall laughed softly to himself before turning to his current task. His mood instantly sobered. Under his breath, he whispered, "I'm sorry, lass. I would take all of this back if I could. I would rewind time if it would fix your future. I promise, as soon as this is over, I will never darken your doorstep again."

If he were a smart man, he'd have insisted on dealing with the water sprite migration. Charlotte Carver was one of the most difficult assignments he'd ever been given. He didn't think straight when she was near her, and now he was talking to himself as if she were standing in front of him—not that he could ever tell her those words to her face.

"Oh, lass, ya deserve better than the hand you've been dealt."

"Charlotte, please answer me!" Lydia's yell disrupted his thoughts. "I can explain."

He hurried through the woods to find her. "Lydia?"

"Niall? Is that you?" Lydia appeared before him on the edge of the trees by her house. She had kind blue eyes and a giving heart. If anyone was going to complement the stubborn personality of his oldest brother, Erik, it was Lydia. "Have you seen Charlotte? She was just here, but she took off. I can't find her."

"What do ya mean, she took off?" Niall quickly stepped toward Lydia's home.

"She knows, Niall! I thought you said erased memories couldn't come back? You all told me that this was for the best, and I believed you. I know what taking in Iain's magick did to her. I know why I can't invite her around when Iain is nearby. I follow all the rules and..." Lydia took a deep, panicked breath and opened her mouth as if to continue her rush of words.

Niall held up a hand to stop her. "What did she say?"

"She knows I've been lying to her." Tears entered Lydia's eyes. "I've done everything I was supposed to do, and now my best friend hates me. She could barely look at me. I should never have trusted you. I should have demanded you left her mind intact. I—"

"Ya are worked up. I will take care of it. Which way did she go?"

"I don't know! Into the woods, I think. I would have seen her if she took the path to town." Lydia reached to grab hold of his arm. The desperation in the gesture took him by surprise. "Niall, please, no more. Don't take anything else from her. I don't want her to hate me, but it was the clearest I've seen her in a long time. Maybe she's coming back to us. Maybe she'll be alright this time."

Niall knew his personality often came off as

gruff and unfriendly. He cleared his throat and did his best to comfort his sister-by-marriage. "I will..."

"You will what?" Lydia asked.

"I give ya my word I will not harm her." He couldn't meet her steady gaze as he slowly pulled his arm from her grip.

Lydia let him go. "Thank you, Niall. I know that goes against your instincts, but I also know you won't break that promise."

"My instincts are to protect the family. That is my sole purpose." Niall let his eyes shift as he looked around the area. "Ya may want to go back inside. I can track her much more easily if I shift forms, and I don't want ya to be frightened of me."

"Niall, you do know that you're more to this family than our protector, don't you?" Lydia leaned to the side, forcing him to meet her gaze.

Lydia meant well, but this was not a subject he wished to speak to her about.

"I won't hurt ya." Despite the assurance, he was prepared to see the fear in her eyes as he released his hold on the wolf. Fur sprouted over his flesh. His bones cracked, breaking as he shifted, and his jaw elongated to fit sharpened teeth. Lydia gasped and he heard her stumbling a few steps away from him. He had known she'd be frightened to see his transformation into the wolf-human hybrid.

Niall fell forward. He would be able to track Charlotte easier in this form, but it would take all of his concentration to make sure other primal instincts didn't try to take hold. It had been a long time since he'd let himself run wild.

He took a deep breath, detecting the faintest trace of her scent before running after her. The fresh air and soft ground felt like freedom, and it tempted him to forget his purpose. That was the trouble with the wolf. Its primal instincts were always ready to take over.

As he moved, other smells caught his attention —the rotting den of the goblin, a nest of *gremains*, the faintest trace of leprechauns and tar. The woods were filled with supernatural traces and he was unable to hold on to Charlotte in the midst of it. He stopped, his chest heaving for breath as he panted from his run. There were nearly eighty acres out here, but she was a human and couldn't get too far on foot.

Even if the wolf shifter enjoyed tracking, as a man, he was overcome with fear that danger would befall her. The woods were not safe, not until he had a chance to clean them up. Niall listened to the forest, to scratches and chirps. The distant beat of Raibeart's feet echoed behind him as the man shuffled through fallen leaves and twigs.

Try as he might, he could not detect Charlotte. She'd simply disappeared.

Chapter Nine

Charlotte stared at Niall, unable to move as she watched him reaching into the air to pop her memories like iridescent bubbles with the tip of his finger. A bonfire burned in the sheriff's lawn—*pop*. Lydia screamed—*pop*. Erik's face shifted into that of a were cat—*pop*.

He paused, watching a memory of when she'd secretly paid for Lacy Baxton's restaurant tab. The woman raised her three siblings like they were her own after their parents died. Only Alana knew about Charlotte doing that. He lowered his finger. Another memory drifted past him, this time of Charlotte dropping off canned goods at a food bank. Then of her reading alone in the park.

"I'm sorry, lass, I would take all of this back if I

could," he whispered. He waved his hand, pushing the bubbles aside, leaving those memories intact as he searched for more.

The image of Charlotte drinking from the poison goblet appeared, followed by others.

Pop.

Pop.

Pop. Pop.

Charlotte gasped and swatted her hands to stop him, only to realize she lay on the ground in the middle of the woods. Statues surrounded her, overgrown with vines in what appeared to be part of an old garden. There was only one place in Green Vallis that would look like this—the MacGregor estate. The property had about six acres of gardens, some of which resembled forests. Weeping willows cried and all sorts of creatures, real and imagined, hid behind moss-covered boulders the size of cars. It wouldn't be unheard of to have a statuary hidden somewhere inside them.

Only...how did she get here?

Not again.

Charlotte touched her head, trying to recall the last thing she remembered before passing out. She'd been so angry at Lydia, but even more hurt by the betrayal. She moaned as she rolled onto her side. Her limbs shook as she tried to push herself up from a broken stone slab partly buried in the ground.

An eerie quiet settled over the chilly woods. She was thankful for the sweater. Tree limbs cast shadows as they blocked the late afternoon sun. Hours must have passed since she left Lydia's. Orange light speckled the ground. The sound of a raven squawked in the distance, only to be answered by another, back and forth as if they had a conversation.

Charlotte stumbled to sit on a stone bench. The statue before her caught her attention. The name "Helena" was carved in the base. The stone was smooth marble, shaping a youthful yet tragic figure. The only mar was the hairline crack across the statue's chest. She recognized the woman it depicted—the English ghost who'd stopped her in the woods.

"You can't trust them. If you do, you'll end up like me, here, in this place."

Charlotte gasped to find the spirit of Helena sitting next to her on the bench. "Who?"

"You don't need me to tell you that. You already know." Helena didn't appear quite like the other spirits Charlotte had seen. There was more animation in her features, and her skin seemed to flow like sand in the wind even when she wasn't moving. "I feel the empty places in you."

"Is this your memorial?"

"It is my trap." Helena faded, only to reappear before her statue. She looked up at herself. "Look at that foolish face."

"I think you look beautiful." Charlotte tried being nice, even as the ghost made her nervous. It was the truth. The statue of the woman appeared delicate and innocent, her waif features awash with sadness and her pose inquisitive; as if asking for reasons why she was frozen in her current form.

Helena began to tremble. The flowing pattern of her skin blew apart, becoming a storm of white mist. When she passed over Charlotte it felt like a blast of sandy heat, not cold like most ghosts.

Charlotte pressed a palm against her chest as her heart squeezed painfully. The discomfort only lasted a few seconds. Helena swirled around the statue, weathering the stone face until it was pitted and malformed.

Simply defacing the statue wasn't enough. Helena shoved it from its pedestal and hovered above the stone as it crashed. She began screaming, a high-pitched, horrible sound that was nothing like the soft accent of moments before.

Charlotte covered her ears and Helena shot off into the forest like a streak of light. The screaming became faint as the ghost flew away.

When the spirit was gone, Charlotte ran down a narrow path leading from the destroyed statue. The path split in two directions and she wasn't sure which to take.

The woods were too quiet. In stark contrast, her breathing sounded abnormally loud because of it. A shiver ran down her spine, bringing with it a feeling of dread. She felt the spooky sensation of being watched by eyes from the depths of the shadows. She shook the eerie feeling as she tried to collect herself.

Charlotte tried to listen to the forest for a clue as to which way to go. A rabbit darted past her feet and she jumped back, startled. She looked to see what had caused the creature to run and decided it might be safest to follow it.

Suddenly, the rabbit came back, running past her toward Helena's statue, as if no direction was safe.

Charlotte didn't move, except for the shaking in her limbs. She started to back up to follow the frightened rabbit away from the dark path. Suddenly, Helena's scream pierced the woods from one direction. Seconds later, the sound of running feet came from the other.

Charlotte moved off the path to hide behind a tree. She hugged close to the bark. The glow of Helena's body lit up the trees as the spirit neared. A growl sounded and then a loud thud. Something heavy was dragged across the dirt and leaves.

She crept around the tree, staying close to the bark as she tried to peek at what was happening. A hairy creature rolled to his feet as if having been pushed to the ground by the spirit. Moonlight caught an elongated snout and fangs. He came up on all fours and growled before lunging at Helena. The animal was bigger than any wolf she'd ever seen, with front arms and shifted from four legs to two with ease as it stood like a man.

"Wolf man," she whispered, unable to keep the surprised word from escaping. Was this another dream or hallucination? Had she stepped out of reality into a bad 1950s horror film, *Wolf Man and the Angry Ghost*? This, after she had just begun to believe she had her sanity back.

The ghost dissipated around the wolf before becoming corporeal. She screeched, an awful sound that forced Charlotte to cover her ears. The wolf howled as if in pain. He slashed a clawed hand, this time making contact. Helena's scream stopped but left a ringing in Charlotte's ears.

The wolf reached back a clawed hand. Light formed a ball in his palm. Helena slammed herself against him and magick shot into the branches. Charlotte cried out in surprise as sparks rained over her. Covering her head, she hurried away from the tree into the cover of another one.

Helena screeched and again flew off into the trees, leaving Charlotte alone with the wolf. Her heart pounded and she closed her eyes tight, willing the animal away. She heard heavy breathing that verged on a growl. When nothing happened, she opened her eyes.

Wolf man stood before her, yellowed eyes watching her as his chest heaved for air.

"Please, don't hurt me. I mean you no harm," she whispered, her shaky voice barely making it past her lips.

The wolf turned from her and fell on all fours. He bent his head forward. A ripple worked over him and a series of awful snaps and pops sounded as his body contorted. Fur retracted into flesh as the animal became human. Charlotte couldn't look away. When the shift was over, a naked man knelt, facing away from her. He didn't have to turn for her to recognize him.

"Niall?" She stared at his back.

His head lifted. The trees shadowed him, but she thought she saw him nod. Jeans appeared on his legs. "Are ya harmed?"

"Terrified, but..." She took a deep breath as relief filled her.

Niall stood and turned to face her. "I promise ya have no reason—"

Charlotte cut off his words as she ran toward him. She buried her face against his naked chest as tears filled her eyes.

He stiffened, not exactly pulling her into his embrace. She didn't care.

"I thought," she tried to speak. "I thought..."

Hesitantly, a hand touched her arm. A second hand found the small of her back. He patted her lightly before holding her a little tighter. His body remained stiff as she pressed against him.

"Lydia was worried when ya ran off and I have been trying to find ya. I'm sorry ya had to see me shifted. I never meant for that to happen, but when I heard the wraith scream, there wasn't a choice but to—"

"Thank goodness that was real." Charlotte lifted her head to look up at him. She became aware of his body against hers, the strength in his arms and chest. She'd always thought Niall handsome—frustrating but handsome. His breath hit her cheek and it was almost as intimate as a kiss. "I thought I was crazy and hallucinating again. I'm tired of not knowing what is real."

"You're not frightened because ya saw me shifted?" He sounded surprised by the fact.

"Oh, you're scary, wolf man," she assured him a little flippantly, but as she admitted it, she knew she hadn't been scared of him. Her nerves tingled where they touched as if trying to awaken more inside her. Her hands rested on his sides, holding him close. The primal energy of his shifted form remained between them as if a caged animal paced beneath his skin. The danger of what he could become should have sent her running, but instead she wanted to see him shift again.

All the moodiness and stubbornness she had seen inside him started to make sense. He held himself under tight rein. While the rest of his family played pranks and games, Niall stood like a watchful guardian. All the times they'd been in the same vicinity, all the things said about him, the feeling she had now while looking into his eyes, even the fact that he'd bought her a buffet of all her favorite takeout foods, they came together like pieces of a puzzle.

She'd misjudged him. Niall wasn't some stubborn ass who cared about nothing and no one. He wasn't some renegade biker who thought only about himself.

The clarity of the moment caused a rush of feelings. She didn't want to let him go, and she didn't know how to express what she thought. The tingling strength of attraction took her by surprise, and warred with the knowledge that he'd erased some of her memories.

Niall's gaze moved to her mouth and he looked as if he wanted to say something more. Instead, he released her and stepped back. A T-shirt magickally appeared on his chest. "Ya should not be out in the forest right now. It's not safe. I'm not even sure how ya came upon this place."

"I don't think that ghost wants to hurt me." Charlotte glanced down the path were Helena had disappeared. She hated that he'd let her go, but had no reason to go back into his arms. "Since Gramma Annabelle appeared to me, I see spirits all the time now."

"It's a wraith, not just a spirit." Niall's eyes flashed with the yellow of the wolf as he looked around the forest. As if deciding it was safe enough to travel, he lifted his hand and gestured that they should leave.

"Well, whatever you call it, I think it's mad at you, not me." For all her bravado, Charlotte kept close to Niall as they walked. She tried to convince herself that what she felt was simply a rush of adrenaline brought on by the supernatural battle she'd witnessed.

Chapter Ten

What in the hell was he thinking? He'd almost kissed Charlotte.

Niall blamed the wolf. Naturally, it had always carried the most primitive, primal, impulsive part of him. When he let it out, it brought with it all the pent-up frustration, locked-up desire, and secret passions he tried to keep buried. The single-minded purpose was great when chasing prey or running for his life. But when the danger was gone, and a beautiful woman stood in his arms, it was another drive altogether. He needed focus to be a hunter. He couldn't have distractions. He couldn't kiss Charlotte. He was meant to protect her and help her and...

If he thought he'd wanted to stop at a kiss, then he was an even bigger fool.

Niall didn't bother to hide the sound of his footsteps as he led her toward the MacGregor mansion. Hopefully the noise would send any supernatural creatures running in the opposite direction. Seeing him lose against a wraith was enough excitement for one evening. It's not that the spirit had gotten the better of him in a fight, but he'd failed to capture it so that meant he lost. He lost because he'd wanted to stay with Charlotte. Otherwise, he'd have given chase.

"What is that smell?" Charlotte asked, her voice strange as she gagged.

He'd been so preoccupied with his attraction for her that he'd walked them straight into the goblin den in the mansion's garden. The mound was crafted out of broken pieces of the dining room table, rusted car parts, shrubbery, and some sort of organic material he didn't want to think too much about. Yellow fungus created a path to the opening of the den, killing all plant life within a few inches of it, and it would continue to spread like a disease if left unchecked. Flies buzzed around the rotting pile. His shifter hearing caught a light snore coming from within. The goblin was home.

Niall held up his finger to his mouth, "*Shh—*"

"Oh, that's awful!" Charlotte exclaimed, not seeing the gesture in time to be quiet. She gagged, before covering her nose and mouth with her hands. "What died? *Ugh.*"

"*Ra-rawr-ar.*" Grumbling sounds came from within. Niall darted toward Charlotte, gathering her in his arms to lift her away from the mound before holding her protectively against him.

"What—?" Her question was cut off by a swarm of fairies that darted out of the mound. The tiny creatures were attracted to the den like flies to compost. This particular species of fairy was gnarled and ugly, things which would bite and sting and pinch and scratch. One on its own was a nuisance which would cause a bad infection with their dirty hands. A horde could do some real damage.

A goblin burst out of the den. The squat creature waddled toward them, carrying with him a smell ten times worse than his home. The fumes were so horrible they distorted the air like heat rising from a desert road. Normally goblins were naked or in tattered clothing, but this one wore his sister's shirt, a gold and white striped number that looked as if it had sequins sewn along the shoulders.

"What is that?" Charlotte demanded, before gasping loudly as the goblin flailed his arms and came after them. She clutched Niall tightly, her legs moving as if she'd crawl up him like a tree.

He swung her out of the way. "Don't let the goblin touch ya. That odor will follow ya for days."

"Ah!" she squeaked and jogged her feet.

Two fairies dove out of formation, tiny claws ready as they aimed for Charlotte's face. Niall batted his hand, sending them flying. One stuck on the side of the fetid mound and the other slammed into a tree and fell to the ground. This did not sit well with the remaining horde, and they proceeded to dive-bomb Niall and Charlotte.

He swept Charlotte into his arms and shielded her with his body. He held her as he retreated toward the house. A fairy stung the back of his neck and he grunted in pain. He dropped Charlotte's legs when they reached the back door and turned to swat the pests.

Charlotte opened the door and pulled the back of his shirt to force him inside. The goblin wobbled toward them with an evil laugh, arms wide as if he expected a hug. When he was through the door, she slammed it shut. A fairy smashed into the glass, creating an almost comical display before sliding down.

"Ugh, I can still smell it." Charlotte plugged her nose.

Niall glanced down to a dark patch on her jeans. "That's not the goblin."

She followed his gaze down and made a noise of disgust. She dug her toe against the heel of her shoes to force them off.

"I told ya not to let him touch ya." He couldn't help laughing.

Charlotte unbuttoned her jeans and shoved them down her hips. She struggled to get them off without touching the goblin handprint. Niall laughed harder.

"I'm glad you think this is so funny," she scoffed. "Your neck looks like you were attacked by a blue bee."

Niall touched the welt on his neck and winced. The fairy had gotten him good. The wound would have a blue coloring to it. Charlotte wrinkled her face and pinched the waist of her jeans. She held them out to him. "Get rid of them."

He obeyed, pausing to make sure he could safely open the door. The fairies had flittered back to their smelly home and the goblin looked confused as he stared up at a sapling. Niall cracked it open and tossed the jeans onto the back lawn. As they landed, the goblin turned. He wobbled over to grab them and then ran back to his mound carrying his new prize.

"Oh," Charlotte said mournfully. She tugged at the hem of her long sweater to cover more of her legs. "I really liked those jeans."

"Don't worry, I have something ya can borrow upstairs." He refused to glance down to where her naked legs poked out from under her sweater.

"Niall?" His mother's voice forced him to turn around. "Why is Charlotte Carver half naked by the garden door? She shouldn't be out in this weather like that."

Margareta MacGregor might have sounded sweet and soft spoken, but he knew the softer his mother's tone, the more annoyed she was. There was plenty to be aggravated about. When she'd left, she'd had a beautiful home. When she came back, it was to find that home looking like her adult children had thrown a supernatural frat party.

"Is she having another of her episodes?" Margareta sighed, as if they didn't have time to deal with yet another problem.

"*She* is not," Charlotte snapped. "*She* is missing her pants because *she* just took a stroll through your lovely goblin garden, where *she* was chased by evil bumblebees after being kidnapped by a wraith."

Margareta frowned. "I can't tell if she's serious or having another mental breakdown? Evil bumblebees?"

"Fairies." Niall pointed at the welt on his neck.

Margareta gave a disapproving shake of her head. "Have Cait put something on that before ya turn blue and I lose any hope of grandkids from ya."

"Aye," he agreed.

"Not that I'm holding out much hope on that front," his mother grumbled to herself, "after nearly five hundred years of waiting."

"Aye," he said again, just to be contrary. It worked; she arched a brow at him and shook her head.

Charlotte tilted her head to look past Margareta toward the dining room.

"Ingrates," his mother scolded. "All of ya. I don't know how I gave birth to nothing but ingrates."

"We must take after Da's side," Niall said. Charlotte coughed as she tried to hide her laugh.

"Aye." Margareta went to the window to look out at the garden. She scowled. "I blame your Da. This mess looks like an Angus MacGregor special."

"Da can't help how he is, but what made ya marry him anyway? Were ya doing penance?" Niall winked at Charlotte.

"There's no accounting for love. When I met your Da, he was tied to a tree limb, half..." She paused and eyed Charlotte.

"Half?" Charlotte prompted.

"Cait said ya were more...clear," Margareta stated, though the words weren't exactly a compliment. "I don't suppose ya are going to start screaming again and pulling at your hair?"

"What happened to your house?" Charlotte asked, matching the woman's tone. She walked toward the dining room.

They had cleaned up some since the last time Niall saw it. A pile of broken table and chair pieces were piled in the corner, ready to be hauled off. The floor, which had been scuffed and broken, now looked polished like new, thanks to magick. The dented walls had also been smoothed and repaired.

However, the light fixture hung on a wire at an odd angle.

Margareta stepped in front of Charlotte to keep her from exploring further. "Are ya tired, dear? Ya look sleepy."

"Ma, leave her. No more magick. She's under my protection." Niall didn't like the sharpened way his mother looked at him, but he didn't drop his gaze.

"Half what?" Charlotte asked.

"Half my heart!" Raibeart announced, sauntering into the room. He paused, and pointed a finger at Niall. "I've got a bone to pick with ya, chicken laddie."

"I see ya chased them off," he answered. "Well fought, Uncle Raibeart."

"Now, don't think I don't know when—*hey!*" Raibeart pointed at Charlotte. "Crazy Charlotte, ya lost your pants."

Charlotte pulled self-consciously at the hem of her long sweater.

"It's too cold for a wee lassie like ya to be out runnin' amuck." Raibeart lifted his arm and waved his hand as if he expected her to fall in line next to him. "Come with me, Crazy Charlotte. I have something ya can wear."

Charlotte looked helplessly at Niall, who quickly intervened. "I've got something for her upstairs."

"Well, get her covered up quick before your brother sees her. Euann is hell bent on marrying this one, and," he shielded his mouth and jutted a thumb at Margareta, "we have enough crazy women in this family."

"Raibeart, I need ya in the back gardens. We have an infestation and need an exterminator," Margareta ordered.

"Never fear, Raibeart loves beer," Raibeart answered.

"Don't you mean, never fear, Raibeart is here?" Charlotte asked.

"Why would I say that? Of course I'm here, but when I get done I'd like beer and whiskey." Raibeart shook his head as he moved to go to the back gardens. He paused to pat Charlotte on the head a few times. "There's a good lassie."

She snapped her teeth at Raibeart's hand, causing him to jerk his fingers back.

Raibeart laughed. "I like a lass with bite."

"Raibeart, exterminate." Margareta pointed the man toward the garden door. "Niall, get Charlotte something more appropriate. See if anything is left in Malina's room."

As Niall escorted her from the dining room, she said, "I'm not loving the nickname Crazy Charlotte."

"Pay Raibeart no mind. He's been hit with the magick stick one too many times," Niall said.

Charlotte paused as she looked around the destroyed front hall of the MacGregor mansion. The wood balusters had broken on the stairs, and the marble floor was still cracked. Wires were swept aside, and not all of Euann's car parts had been picked up. There was a steering wheel leaning against the stairs.

However, the chandelier that had been in the middle of the floor was now magickally repaired and hanging as if nothing had happened. Niall guessed Cait had something to do with that. She loved antiques and would have made it a priority.

"Hey, Charlotte, nice pants." Malina snickered as she crossed from the storage room beneath the stairs toward the dining room. His sister might have appeared casual, but Malina only materialized the best designer clothes. She had the power to make anything from a picture, except living things. His new sisters-in-law had been eating their way through an entire catalog of desserts once they'd found out Malina's materialized food had no nutritional value or calories.

"I like your husband's decorating," Niall countered by way of defending Charlotte from being teased. He gestured at the crack in the floor.

Malina scrunched up her face. "Better than you could do. I've seen your apartment."

"Ma's in there," Niall said as Malina tried to pass into the dining room. His sister instantly stopped, reversed three steps, and then turned to hurry back the way she'd come.

"So, seriously, what was your mom about to say? Tied to a tree limb, half...?" Charlotte asked.

"My ma claims my da was stuck in a tree, half-shifted into a bird because he and my uncle Fergus messed up a spell, and she was forced to rescue him. My da said he transformed into a bird to sing to another woman before he saw my ma, and that she tells her version of the story because she's jealous. I'm sure the truth is in there somewhere." Niall hovered his hand near the small of her back and urged her to join him on the staircase. "They've been married a long time, and I've seen them argue like it, but their love runs deep."

"How long have they been married?" she asked.

"A long time." As they neared the top of the stairs, Niall gestured toward the room he kept at the mansion. He had never slept in it, but Malina made sure it had a bed and a change of clothes. It was smaller than the other rooms, but had its own bathroom. Clothes were strewn over the floor from where ghosts had thrown things around. He gestured at them. "Take your pick."

Charlotte stumbled toward his messy bed, ignoring the clothes. Without a word, she crawled into it and collapsed. Seconds later, he heard the soft sounds of her even breathing. She'd fallen asleep.

Niall watched her for a long moment before doing something he'd rarely done in his life. He swept his hand over the room, using his magick to straighten up in hopes of impressing a woman. Drawers open and clothes folded themselves before settling into place. The fire lit in the fireplace to give her warmth. His bedding slithered over Charlotte, covering her up. He even mended the cracks in the wall.

The painting of him someone had hung on the wall over the small fireplace straightened. It was of a different time. Not better or simpler, just differ-ent. Well, perhaps it had been better for his kilt, as it had yet to see the tatters of time. The Scottish scene behind him had been embellished by the artist, now long dead, but it sufficiently reminded him of his childhood.

"So many years," he whispered, thinking of the centuries that had passed. He rarely stopped long enough to think of them, to feel them weighing on his shoulders. There were so few pleasures left to him, but tonight he'd laughed. Half-naked Char-lotte had made him laugh and forget the duties before him. She'd lightened that weight for a few moments.

The bed was large enough to fit both of them, so he lay down next to her to listen to the sounds of her breathing. He stayed atop of the covers and told himself it was to watch over her, but deep down he knew she'd be safe with his family cleaning up below. Each of her breaths were like a song on the distant wind; he wanted to hear more, but it wasn't his music to listen to. Charlotte was not his, would never be. She deserved so much more than an ill-tempered warlock who hunted the supernatural in a tattered kilt.

Chapter Eleven

"Here we go again," Charlotte muttered as she opened her eyes to a strange location. A fire caught her attention, and when her tired brain determined it wasn't a bonfire fueled by possessed townsfolk, she wondered what new memory she was experiencing.

A fireplace cast an orange light over a dresser. The flames danced and she looked for shadowed creatures on the wall. They did not appear. The light around a curtain was barely discernable along the edges. Her skin tingled and her naked legs moved restlessly under silky sheets. Her foot bumped something hard and she pushed her toes down the length of a shin.

This memory wasn't frightening. Why would they take it away from her?

A familiar scent caused her to turn. Her hand lifted as if following instinct. She didn't bother to control her actions. Why would she? If this was something that already happened, the best she could do is relive it.

Blankets kept her skin from the man next to her. She snuggled closer. Her fingers found a stubbled jaw and she had no intention of stopping. She lifted her mouth to kiss Niall.

Niall?

Why was she kissing Niall? And why was he kissing her back? How did something like this happen?

The questions swirling in her mind did not stop her actions. She parted her lips to invite a deeper kiss. He took the invitation and slipped his tongue along the seam of her mouth. A strong hand rested on her hip, kneading her through the blanket.

Her mouth opened wider and his responded in kind. Her legs become even more restless, moving beneath the covers to be free. She delved her hands into his hair before pulling them down over his cheek and neck. She hated his shirt for stopping her exploration of skin even as she skimmed over it feel lower. Each ridge and valley of his chest became a defined adventure as she worked her way to his waist.

Niall moaned into her mouth, uttering some Gaelic phrase that she couldn't understand. The words wove over her and she wasn't sure if it was passion or a spell that made her shiver. She pushed a knee over his thigh, but the sheets restricted her movements as she tried to pin him to her.

Niall dug his hands beneath the blankets, down her back before finally settling over her cotton panties. Heat seemed to pulse from his fingers, causing a small shockwave of desire to tighten her stomach. Being a warlock gave him an unfair advantage, but she wasn't complaining.

Charlotte couldn't stop kissing him, not that she wanted to stop. She remembered the beast of his transformation and that only made the moment all that much hotter. She imagined she felt that wild animal beneath the surface, desperate to be freed. She squirmed, pulling the covers until finally she worked the barrier from between their bodies.

Her hands moved as if possessed. They found his jeans, pulling and tugging until the button was freed and the zipper down. He didn't wear underwear, so it was easy for her to cup his ass and squeeze. His skin was so firm, and so warm.

"Char—" He tried to speak but she cut him off by reaching to feel his arousal. To her pleasure, she found him as ready as she. His eyes began to glow with a golden light.

She pushed her panties off her hips and hooked her legs over his thigh to turn him on top of her. His jeans slid lower but trapped his knees together. Her sweater bunched around her waist. The material became hot, but there were more pressing matters for her to attend to.

Charlotte spread her legs and wiggled her hips, finding the perfect angle. Her body teased the tip of his shaft, jerking with the first intimate contact. Niall bit his lip, the look was sensual even as he tried to stop himself. She pushed her hips higher, willing him to move, to plunge, to join her in her primal search for release.

"Niall, come on," she whispered. "Are we going to do this or what?"

Niall answered with a hard thrust. He filled her completely and she cried out in surprise.

There was no turning back. His heavy breath mingled with hers. His eyes glowed like a wild beast and he moved like a man unable to stop himself.

There was no room for logic in a moment like this. She wanted to be with him, and she needed the release he offered.

Their fevered bodies met in frantic thrusts. When climax came, it was a visceral experience. Charlotte tensed, feeling months of frustration flowing out of her limbs to leave her weak and more relaxed than she'd been in a very, very long time.

"Why did you erase that one?" she whispered, rubbing her cheek. She waited for the moment she'd stop hallucinating the past and come back to reality.

"I don't understand." Niall pushed his pants off his legs and tossed them aside.

"This memory, why did you..." Charlotte pushed up on the bed and looked at him questioningly. "This feels like it's really happening."

"Lass, ya are not making much sense." Niall lifted his hand to her forehead as if to check her temperature. He sat up then placed a finger on her forehead and another on her cheekbone as if to hold her eyelids open.

She leaned back and swatted at his fingers. "Stop that."

"Where are we?" he asked, his expression worried.

Charlotte glanced around as she tried to remember. Her eyes fell on a disturbingly large painting of Niall standing in front of a castle landscape like some Scottish historical romance hero with a sword. "Your bedroom in the MacGregor mansion."

"What happened today?"

"We had sex," she stated.

"Before that," he insisted.

"Seriously? You really need to work on your pillow talk." Charlotte gave a wry laugh. "Fine. You finally confessed to messing around with my brain. I went to Lydia's, argued with Gramma Annabelle, quit my job because I was hurt by my best friend lying to me. A wraith kidnapped me to warn me against the MacGregor family, and part of me thinks she might have a point, even if she did start screeching like some hell spawn."

He tried to interrupt, but she held up her hand.

"Let me finish. You turned into a werewolf and fought the wraith. We were attacked by goblins and you got a blue hickey from a fairy. We came up here, and had great sex, and you're about to make some kind of lame excuse as to why we can't ever do it again."

"Well, uh..." His eyes dipped down.

"I get it." Charlotte had never been clearer than she was in that moment. Her mind felt sharp and focused. "You're the moody MacGregor, standing in the background, passing silent judgment while being saddled with responsibility. Everyone else gets to goof off and have fun and for some reason, you're the one they send off to battle evil elves, or exorcise jinn, or chase down rogue killer werewolves in the Carpathian Mountains and—"

Charlotte's world instantly flashed with black and she found herself surrounded by rocks and trees. The air in her lungs felt thin as she looked down from the top of a mountain over a rugged landscape. A pink and yellow sunset spread over the distance. It was one of the most beautiful views she had ever seen.

A loud growl of warning sounded and she turned toward the darkness behind her. Yellow eyes stared from the trees before a wolf ran along the cliff away from her. With a crash, two larger wolf shifters rolled before her. She yelped in surprise. Unlike the first, these were not regular wolves, one was Niall and the other a man just like him, but with gray fur. Wounds, bleeding and raw, covered their bodies, signifying they had been fighting.

Her legs locked and she couldn't run or look away. She tried to speak, but knew this was not a memory she belonged in.

Niall's claws sliced into flesh. The gray werewolf howled in pain. They fought viciously, slashing at each other with deadly intent. The longer she stared at Niall, the more she felt what he felt. Her body ached and burned. She felt blood trickle were there was only uninjured flesh. Beyond the physical injuries, she felt determination hiding fear. The gray werewolf had been around, hunting this forest since before Vlad the Impaler ruled Wallachia. He was a bloodthirsty adversary who killed people with an indiscriminate hunger. Her heart pumped wildly and she wanted to strike out. The werewolf had to be stopped.

The gray werewolf rolled on top of Niall, pinning him down. Fangs clamped down on Niall's neck. Charlotte knew this might be the end. Somehow, though, Niall managed to free a hand and stabbed his claws into the gray werewolf's neck. By some miracle, Niall wobbled to his feet and the gray wolf lay dead. The shift began to leave his body, fur retracting and claws shortening.

"*Omoara-l*," a hunter yelled, charging from the woods with a rifle drawn. He led two others. *Kill it.*

Niall was weak from the fight and didn't stand a chance against the round of bullets. He stumbled back, mid-shift. She reached to him, but her hand went through him like a ghost visiting his past. Niall fell off the side of the cliff, his arms flailing as he disappeared into the darkness.

Chapter Twelve

Niall held Charlotte's limp body in his arms. She felt hot to the touch and so he'd pulled the sweater off her. One moment she'd been ranting at him, saying things she could not have known, and the next she was trembling on the bed, having a seizure.

After the tremors stopped, he held her and waited. That is when the guilt set in. He should not have made love to her. Though she spoke with newfound strength, and accepted the supernatural events she had lived through, she was still fragile. He should have been stronger. When she kissed him, he should have been able to resist.

Fool that he was, he knew if she were to kiss him again, he'd succumb to her. That said, he wasn't foolish enough to believe she had actually wanted to be with him. There were many more plausible explanations as to why she'd kissed him. Her body craved his magick to fill in the missing pieces. Or the potion the *lidérc* gave her had residual effects and made her try to pull life from him. Or...or...

"Tell me how to fix this for ya, Charlotte." Niall tried to bury the burden of his feelings. "Tell me how to make it better. I don't know *how* ya see the truth, or how those memories have come back, but I am glad they have."

Charlotte gasped and flailed in his arms. He held her loosely, letting her move while trying to keep her from injuring herself. She smacked him across the face. Her eyes opened in surprise at what she'd done, blinking rapidly as she looked around for any possible backlash to her unseemly behavior.

"Niall," she whispered, pushing up from the bed. Charlotte reached for his shoulder, finding a scar from when he'd been shot. She then pulled back the covers to expose his naked thigh to check a second bullet wound. The delicate way her fingers pressed at his skin caused his body to react and he couldn't hide his growing arousal. When she moved to his stomach, he realized what she was looking for.

Niall grabbed her hand. "What are ya doing?"

"I saw them shoot you." Her gaze again strayed toward his scars. "How did you survive falling off the cliff? What about that gray werewolf you were fighting? I remember standing there thinking he was older than you, and this is going to sound insane, but that he was around since before Vlad the Impaler became ruler of that place... I can't remember what it was called now."

"Wallachia," he supplied. The comment about Vlad the Impaler was exactly what a local had told him when he was asking about the gray wolf legend in the area. How could she know that?

"That's it." Charlotte sighed with relief. "It was weird. For some reason, it was like we were in Eastern Europe, but I've never been to Eastern Europe, have I?"

"Not with me." Niall didn't understand what was happening. Charlotte remembering her own past was one thing, but to remember an event that only he and a few Romanian hunters knew about?

"And the hunter said something, and I understood him," she continued. "Omora? Omoah?"

"*Omoara-l,*" Niall said.

"Right." She nodded. "It means...I knew what it meant."

"Kill it." Niall pulled the covers over his lap to hide the evidence of his desire for her.

"So how did I learn to speak...?"

"Romanian." He sighed, not liking that she knew all this about that night.

"I speak Romanian?" She moved her mouth as if trying to get the foreign language to come back to her.

"No. I do." Niall saw her shiver, and he lifted his hand to stoke the fireplace without bothering to get out of bed. The fire burned brighter. "Ya were looking at a memory from my past."

"So, was that gray wolf really like a thousand years old?" she asked.

"More like six hundred," he corrected. "I didn't stop to ask him about his birthday."

"Wow. I guess I never thought that..." Her eyes widened and she looked at him. "How old are you?"

"Old," he mumbled.

"No, really. When were you born?"

"1655."

"Wow." Charlotte's mouth dropped open a

little before she started laughing. "Never mind, you really are old. And the rest of your family?"

"I'm the youngest sibling," he said.

"Wow."

"Ya keep saying that," he muttered, suddenly feeling those hundreds of years.

"It's just that I would have assumed you were the oldest by the way you act all protective. Aren't the youngest children supposed to be the carefree, wild ones?" Her smile was infectious.

"Ya don't think I'm carefree?" The very idea of such a word being applied to him was comical in its absurdity.

"I think you're," she paused and her smile fell into something more thoughtful, "burdened."

"I'm not burdened," he lied.

"I disagree. When we were in Romania—"

"Ya somehow peeked in at one of my memories. I'm not sure how. I was in the Carpathian Mountains. Alone." Niall glanced at his mansion bedroom, reminded of where they were. She touched his chest and he tensed. He held his breath, feeling her touch like an electrical shock through his system.

"I should be mad at you," she said softly.

"Ya have every right. I should not have taken advantage of ya," Niall agreed.

"The sex?" Charlotte laughed. "I'm pretty sure I took advantage of *you*. But let me give you a heads-up. That was the most fun I've had in a long time. I'll probably try to retake advantage sometime soon."

Pleasure filled him at her words, and he did his best not to appear too eager. It was difficult enough not staring at her in her bra, knowing that beneath the covers she still had not bothered to put on her panties.

"What I meant was, I should be mad at you for taking my memories, and lying to me, and being an asshole, and for being a slumlord...but I'm not. I find I can't be, and I can't explain it." She studied him and arched a brow. "Actually, that's a lie. I *am* mad about the slumlord part."

"I'm not a slumlord," he defended. "I have workers going through fixing everything they can find. I even ordered ya a new bed to replace the damaged one in your apartment."

"You did?"

"Aye. Dar hit the family with bad luck when I was away on a hunt and that spilled over onto our properties in town. Lydia's house was hit by *gremains.* This house was hit with ghosts, goblins, demons, amongst other things. Our apartment building was plagued with broken pipes and bad wiring, and...oh, crap."

"What?"

"*Gremains.*" He sighed in frustration. "Bad plumbing, bad wiring, broken generator...we probably have one hiding out in the building somewhere. It'll keep breaking things until I catch it."

"Is that a kind of gremlin?"

"Aye." Niall sat up on the bed, mentally listing all the things he needed to take care of. "They're mischievous little pains in the arse that like to disassemble anything mechanical or electrical, basically anything that can be taken apart."

"What is it? What's wrong? Why did your expression go all," Charlotte gestured at his face, "dark and gloomy?"

"I shouldn't be lying around. My ma sent Uncle Raibeart to deal with the fairies and goblins, so either he's tied up and trapped inside a goblin's den or engaged to a fairy. Either way, he'll need rescuing. I'll get the *gremain* out of the apartment building, but there is at least one more in the forest who will be looking for a new home to destroy. The hauntings can wait, except for that wraith. It's going to be tricky figuring out why she's here."

"This is what I mean when I say you're burdened," Charlotte said. "Surely Raibeart can take care of himself."

Niall wasn't so sure. How his uncle managed to survive each year was a mystery.

"Fine, if not himself, then surely someone else in the family can look after him."

"They could, but Malina is busy reconciling with Dar and probably trying to avoid our ma. Margareta won't lend a hand. She and Cait hate goblins. Erik will be helping at Lydia's. That leaves Rory and Euann, and those two would end up captured next to Raibeart because they probably couldn't stop bickering long enough to get the job done."

"I think maybe you're underestimating your family," she said.

"I didn't say they weren't capable, I just know from experience they'll come to me to take care of it." Niall made a move to sit up. He didn't want to leave her, but he knew he should.

"Wait." Her hand on his arm stopped him, keeping him on the bed more effectively than a petrifying spell. He felt her move on the bed behind him. Her hand moved up his arm to his face, turning his cheek to look at her.

"I don't regret what we did. For some reason, I think you might." Charlotte's eyes gazed into his. Hope filled him at her words, tempting him with dreams he never allowed himself to have. "We clearly do not get along on a day-to-day basis, and I'm not saying we should go steady or anything, but you have to admit the sex was great. We're both adults. I may be delusional about a lot of things in my life, but I know what this is. You don't love me, and that's okay. I don't expect you to. I'm not asking for romantic dinners and promises, but if we enjoy—"

"Ya want us to be lovers." He tried to condense her point to get her to stop talking about it. All the pleasure he felt faded at her notion of what he felt, and what they could be to each other.

"Why not?" She smiled. Damn, but it was a beautiful smile.

I would let ya see the truth if that meant ya would look at me once the way I see ya every day.

The words from the past whispered through his mind, but he would never say them, not when she was conscious and looking at him.

When he didn't readily answer, she added,

"Maybe the sex was so good *because* we're always arguing."

"And how would this arrangement work?" The idea of his family finding out that Charlotte wanted to use him for his body but nothing else didn't settle well with him. His siblings would tease him relentlessly about it, and each time he'd be reminded of what he couldn't have.

"Well, you see, when a girl likes a boy," she moved to her knees and kissed the corner of his mouth, "and when a boy likes a girl," she kissed him again.

"I meant other people," he explained, resisting the temptation to throw her down on the bed and continue the game she'd started.

"Oh." Her expression fell somewhat. "I mean, I suppose, if you wanted, you could be with other..."

The words hit him worse than the time he'd been kicked in the gut by a possessed donkey. "I meant, do we tell other people?"

She looked at him for a long moment before shaking her head. "I don't think it's anyone else's business what we do."

He desired her almost as much as he wanted to yell at her. This woman was the most frustrating, stubborn, aggravating...

Charlotte kissed him, cutting off all thoughts. He felt the warmth of her tongue poking between his lips. He was hers to command.

Niall ran his hand up her thigh, pulling her so that she fell back onto the mattress. He tugged her bra strap to free a breast. Just as his mouth was lowering, voices invaded from the outside hall. He paused, lips hovering over a tight nipple.

"Erik, no, I don't care what you say right now," Lydia's said from outside his door. "She's my best friend, and I can't stand that she thinks I wanted to hurt her. I need to make sure she's all right and that your family didn't try to petrify her again or—"

Niall pulled his mouth away. Both he and Charlotte glanced toward the door.

"Lydia, wait—" Erik protested.

"She can hate me all she wants, but I'm going to check on her," Lydia said sternly. Charlotte gasped and scrambled beneath him to get up.

Niall lifted his hand to magickally turn the latch in the door to lock Lydia out. He rolled to the side and reached for his jeans. The doorknob jiggled. He didn't have time to dress the usual way; he waved his hand over his body, materializing the clothes to hide his nakedness.

"Help," Charlotte whispered. She'd righted her

bra and was rummaging around the bed for her sweater.

"Open it," Lydia demanded. "Your brother better not be messing with her thoughts again. He promised me that he wouldn't harm her."

Niall magickally dressed Charlotte in one of his old T-shirts and sweatpants. They were too big for her, but at least they were clean. She grabbed her sweater and threw it toward the corner of the room before trying to smooth the covers.

"Open it, or so help me, Erik MacGregor, I'll lay a hand on you and suck all your magickal power out and do it myself," Lydia said.

The door unlocked.

"Thank you," Lydia huffed. "Now move."

Charlotte pushed her hair back. Niall stood beside the bed.

Lydia pushed into the room. "Charlotte, I know you're in here. I need to talk to you."

Charlotte pretended to yawn.

"I know you're mad at me, but I can—" Lydia skidded to a stop as she saw Niall was also in the room. "Niall, what did you do? I told you, we can't take anything else from her. It's not right. I shouldn't have let you in the first place."

"I didn't," Niall protested.

"He didn't," Charlotte said at the same time. "In fact, he's the only one who's told me the truth."

"She remembers everything," Niall said.

"Hey, sorry about the intrusion." Erik appeared from behind his wife. His gaze moved over Charlotte and his brother before going to the floor. He tried to pull Lydia's arm. "*Fíorghrá,* we should let Charlotte rest."

"No, not until she forgives me." Lydia stepped deeper into the room. "Char, please, I'm so sorry. I wanted to tell you everything."

"Maybe I should go." Niall started to leave, but Erik was staring at him strangely and he stopped.

Lydia teared up and sniffed. "I'm sorry. Please, Char, you can't hate me. I didn't know how to help you. When you saw Erik shift on my lawn, you were so freaked out. You started babbling about aliens and all kinds of crazy things. Then later, when Brad and Joe took us to Sheriff Johnson's house, you nearly died by taking in Iain's magick. I think you *might* have died. I would have agreed to anything to have you back. You haven't even been able to go near Iain without the both of you feeling sick. Please, you can't hate me! You can't quit our friendship. You must forgive me. I love you. You're the sister I never had."

"Of course, I forgive you." Charlotte tossed the covers aside and slid off the bed. She caught the waistband of the sweatpants with a fist to keep them from falling.

Lydia hurried to give Charlotte a hug. "I love you so much."

"I love you, too," Charlotte answered. "I was just angry earlier and needed time to try to sort things out."

"Well, I'll tell you everything." Lydia smiled, even as tears wet her cheeks. "I *want* to tell you everything."

Charlotte went in for another hug, but Lydia stopped and looked down.

Niall glanced around the side of the bed to find Lydia standing on Charlotte's discarded underwear. Lydia lifted her foot and frowned. She looked first at Charlotte and then over at Niall.

"We should let Charlotte rest," Erik said. It was then Niall realized his brother had spotted the underwear when he walked in and had instantly suspected what had happened.

"Charlotte?" Lydia asked. She looked at her friend and then Niall again. "Are you...? Did you...?"

Charlotte looked helplessly at him.

"Are you sleeping with Niall?" Lydia blurted, as if she couldn't believe such a fantastical thing. "But, I thought you hated him?" Lydia turned to Niall. "I thought you hated her?"

"We should go." Erik grabbed Lydia a little more forcibly and pulled her with him. "Charlotte, I'm happy to see you're feeling better. Lydia and I would love it if ya came by the house as soon as you're able. I'm sure there is much for ya two to talk about."

"But..." Lydia said in shock. Erik managed to get her out of the room, pulling the door shut as they left. Through the door, he heard Lydia say, "But they don't like each other!"

"So much for keeping it a secret." Charlotte gave a small laugh.

"Yeah, I should go take care of those things before..." Niall's words trailed off as he followed Lydia and Erik out of the room. He couldn't listen to another of Charlotte's definitions of their just-secret-lovers relationship status.

He hid around a corner until he was sure Lydia and Erik had left. He didn't want to explain, especially when he didn't know the answers himself.

Chapter Thirteen

"Okay, spill it." Lydia placed a plate of spaghetti and meatballs down on the table in front of Charlotte. "How did this happen?"

"Where's Erik?" Charlotte asked.

"I sent him away. I wanted time to talk, just us," Lydia answered.

"Is this Gramma Annabelle's secret spaghetti recipe?" Charlotte leaned over to look closer at the plate.

"The secret is pimiento and a pinch of nutmeg," Lydia dismissed.

She knew Lydia wanted details about Niall, but at the same time, Charlotte didn't know what to say about what had happened.

As Charlotte had gone on and on, trying to tell

Niall what he wanted to hear, she kept hoping he'd stop her. Instead, he nodded as if her proposal to be secret lovers was a good one.

Idiot. Of *course* she didn't want a relationship without feelings involved. Of course she felt more when Niall touched her than she let on. Of course she wanted romantic dinners and dates and walks in the moonlight that didn't include goblins or wraiths. Just thinking of him made her tremble with mixed emotions.

"Now spill," Lydia said. "How in the world did you start dating Niall MacGregor? I thought you couldn't stand him. When did this happen?"

"Gramma is not going to be happy you told her secret family recipe." Charlotte picked up a fork and twirled it in the pasta.

"I guess you and Niall make sense, in a way." Lydia tried to force Charlotte to look at her. Charlotte shoved the spaghetti into her mouth to keep from having to answer.

Lydia knew her better than anyone. In many ways, they were opposites, but those differences seemed to fill a place within the other, making them best friends. Lydia had always been reserved. Charlotte had been known to speak first and think later. As girls, Lydia wouldn't stand up for herself when being teased by the other kids about her grandmother being the "Witch on the Hill." Charlotte had been sent to detention more than once sticking up for Lydia. But when Charlotte had a problem, Lydia had always been the first one trying to solve it.

"Niall always comes off a little gruff, but I never thought him capable of..." Lydia took a deep breath. "Char, did he hurt you? Because family or not, I promise Erik will make sure he pays."

Charlotte twirled the fork, loading it with pasta before slowly setting it down. She placed her hands on her lap. "The MacGregors, I get. They were protecting their family and their supernatural secret. I spazzed out when I saw Erik shift, and—"

"Sweetie, it was more than spazzing out. You had a nervous breakdown."

"Fine. I had a nervous breakdown when I saw Erik shift and throw magick balls at his sister," she amended, "but that doesn't explain why you never told me what was happening. I would have believed you. I might not have remembered it happening, but I would have believed you if you'd told me."

"I wanted to tell you everything," Lydia said. She sat down at the table and reached forward. Her arm slid the spaghetti plate aside as she offered her hands to Charlotte.

"But you didn't." Charlotte didn't take Lydia's hands. She clutched hers in her lap, weaving the fingers tightly together. "I thought I had something seriously wrong with me, Lyd. I was terrified I was clinically insane, or had some kind of brain tumor. The doctors couldn't explain why I was losing time, having seizures, why I would have these nightmares and wake up with a knife on my nightstand. I started locking myself in my apartment with these elaborate obstacles just so I wouldn't sleepwalk into the halls and stab a neighbor. I'd see shadow figures dancing on the walls. Ghosts started talking to me and I couldn't tell if they were really there or if I was just hallucinating. I knew Gramma Annabelle was really here, but that didn't mean the others were."

"Why didn't you tell me you were worried about your health?" Lydia scolded. "Doctors? How many did you go to?"

"Five. I didn't want you to worry." Charlotte finally lifted her hands to take Lydia's. "You have been so happy with Erik and starting your new life and I didn't want to bog you down with my stuff."

"Dammit, Charlotte." Lydia leaned forward for

a hug. "New friend rule. If you think you have a brain tumor, you tell me. Got it? I had no idea it was that bad. I thought you were just spacy from the magick."

"Fine. But if some warlock erases part of my brain, you tell me," Charlotte countered. She let go and Lydia sat back in the chair.

"So, Niall." Lydia gave her a pointed look. "I mean, I do sort of get the two of you. He doesn't seem like he scares too easily, and you can rip a guy of his masculine pride with just a sentence and a look."

"Ha ha," Charlotte drawled sarcastically. "Thanks a lot."

"How many times have you sat at this very table and made me listen to your speech on how men weren't confident anymore?" Lydia reached for Charlotte's plate and slid it in front of her again. "How did you put it? There are no warriors left in the world who fiercely protect their women. Society has driven fear into men, and something-something base urges are no longer allowed to something."

"If I said all that, I'm an idiot." Charlotte vaguely recalled saying something along those lines, but what did she know? It's not like she had any serious relationship experience. "You make it sound like I advocated wanting a caveman to hit a woman over the head and drag her away to a cave."

"I don't remember a caveman being part of your theory, but I will say you knew Erik and I were meant to be together before I even did." Lydia smiled and stood to get herself a plate of food. She sat next to Charlotte at the table. "I've missed you."

"I've missed being me," Charlotte admitted. "Now, tell me everything that happened when I was busy being crazy. Don't leave a single thing out."

Chapter Fourteen

"Lydia sent me to find out what your intentions are with Charlotte."

Niall frowned at Erik's words, as he kept his eyes on the goblin's burning den. It was his excuse for refusing to look up at his brother, who spoke to him in Gaelic, as if that would somehow force Niall to answer. He didn't.

The orange flames turned the den to ash while killing most of the smell. As suspected, Raibeart had become distracted from his task. He'd managed to send several of the fairies through the veil, but then wandered off before the job was done.

"I'm curious myself," Erik insisted.

Niall lifted his hands as he concentrated magick in his palms. "Help me smother this fire."

Erik took control of the weather, forcing the air to stir toward him as he stole the oxygen from the flames. Niall pushed his power at the fire, and together they stifled it.

"Good riddance," Erik muttered. "I'm not sure what to think about this new brother of ours. I can't believe ya didn't tell any of us that Malina married a guy in Vegas in the sixties. Though, I'll give him this much, Dar entered the family with a bang."

"I'm not sure I'd call attacking us with bad luck a *bang*," Niall grumbled. Sure, it was easy for everyone else to laugh it off, but it was Niall who had to go hunt down a wraith and make sure nothing else was roaming the forest. All the others had to do was a little magickal housekeeping.

"Ya know what I mean," Erik dismissed. "What else can I help with?"

The offer took Niall by surprise. He picked up a messenger bag from the ground and looped it over his head. "Ya can get Iain to put in the putting green."

"I've been trying. I was thinking this town needs a good golf course," Erik agreed. He kicked the remains of the goblin den, knocking down what little frame remained.

"In the coming days, we'll have to watch for

other dens, but if we keep burning them the goblin will lose interest and move deeper into the earth to hibernate."

Erik's phone rang and he pulled it from his back pocket. "Hello, my beautiful."

Niall glanced at his brother, hiding his jealousy. He also suspected his brother might rescind the offer to help for the lovelier company of his wife. Lydia had complete control over Erik, and she didn't even seem to realize it...which was probably a good thing.

Erik's easy smile fell. "Are ya sure?" His eyes moved to Niall. "Thank ya for calling me, my love. Ya did right. Let me know if ya learn anything more. I love ya."

As Erik lowered the phone, Niall demanded, "Is it Charlotte? Is she hurt?"

"Do ya know she saw the wraith?" Erik asked.

Niall relaxed as he realized Lydia was probably overreacting. He adjusted his messenger bag and absently laid his hand against it to feel the bulge of familiar contents inside. "Aye. I know all about the wraith. Charlotte was in the forest when I fought it. I have it handled. I'm heading out to hunt it down."

"Ya seem concerned about Charlotte." Erik

studied him. "What exactly is happening between the two of ya?"

"She's my responsibility," Niall dismissed. He walked into the trees, hoping that would be the end of the questions. He led the way down a cobblestone path, away from the house. Several of the plants were dormant from the wintery weather.

"I know we walked in on something more than naptime. As the eldest brother, I am ordering ya to answer me. What is the nature of your relationship with Charlotte?" Erik ran ahead of Niall to block the path as he crossed his arms over his chest.

"Ask the elders, they assigned me to take care of her." Niall absolutely did not want to talk about relationships and feelings with Erik. He pushed past his brother.

"Then tell me she means nothing to ya, just a job," Erik said.

Niall stopped and turned to do just that, but couldn't force the lie out.

Erik's teasing grin fell into a look of amazement. "Holy crap, ya can't say it, can ya?"

"I'm not humoring ya," Niall dismissed.

"Niall the Neanderthal, in love," Erik teased. "Wait until I tell—"

Niall marched faster through the forest. Where was a good wraith attack when he needed one?

The wind picked up and a tree limb cracked above his head. Niall looked up in time to see a thick branch break free. He jumped back before it landed on him. His path was now blocked.

"Talk to me," Erik insisted. The wind died down under his command. "I know it's not natural for ya to have a conversation that's more than a few words long, but I am your brother. What's going on in that head of yours? If ya like Charlotte, everyone in the family will be happy for ya. We want ya to find some kind of peace and stop this incessant need to hunt and do your duty."

"I am not obsessive," Niall denied.

"I said incessant." Erik touched his shoulder. "Niall, please, talk to me."

"It's not some incessant need to go out and chase down supernatural problems. Someone in this family has to take care of these things and I don't see any of ya volunteering to clean out a vampire den or fight a siren. It is me the elders order to the hunt. When Malina ran off, they sent me to bring her back. When some distant cousin calls about a killer werewolf, they send me to investigate. When mysterious earthquakes hit Oklahoma, they send me to clean out the leprechaun infestation." Niall didn't bother to hide his aggravation.

"Is this about Helena? We have learned a lot since those days. We've taken precautions with Charlotte. Everyone is watching over her. Hell, Euann is even willing to marry her if—"

Niall turned and grabbed his brother by his shirt. He lifted him up off the ground and growled. "Ya will keep out of my business."

Realizing that the wolf was trying to emerge, he instantly dropped his brother and swung his arm toward the fallen branch. He drew power from the surrounding trees to magickally lift the obstacle out of his way and throw it aside so he could continue on. He ran down the path to make better time as he listened to the distance for signs of the supernatural.

"Fine." Erik kept pace behind him. "We don't have to talk about Charlotte, but we should come up with a plan to deal with Helena."

At that, Niall stopped running. Intense emotions filled him—guilt, fear, dread. "What *about* Helena?"

"Ya said ya knew," Erik answered. He wasn't

the least bit winded from their run. "The wraith that took Charlotte into the forest was Helena."

Niall felt as if the entire world stopped in that moment. His mind raced as he thought of what Charlotte had said. She kept saying a wraith kidnapped her, but he'd thought she was just being overly dramatic to make a point, as women sometimes did. Having a wraith lure someone into the forest wasn't unheard of, or even surprising, but Helena? Why, after all these years?

"Ya didn't know?" Erik whispered.

"What else did your wife tell ya?" Niall insisted. Helena was free? This changed everything.

"Helena somehow led Charlotte to her statue and then warned her against trusting any MacGregor. Helena told Charlotte that they would share the same fate."

"I was so focused on the attack that I didn't stop to think it happened by Helena's statue." Niall frowned. Well, he'd actually been so focused on not kissing Charlotte that he'd not bothered to pay attention to anything else. This just proved he wasn't meant for relationships. If the mere thought of Charlotte knocked him off his game, he wouldn't be able to do his job effectively. "Charlotte didn't mention Helena. She just said the wraith kidnapped her. I thought she might have been mixing up memories again."

"Charlotte didn't seem too bothered by the warning if she went home with ya," Erik offered. "It's possible she didn't believe anything Helena had to say, if that is what has ya so worried."

"I'm not worried," Niall lied. The wind began to whistle in the trees. He glanced at his brother to see if Erik was about to drop another branch on him.

"Not me." Erik searched the surrounding area.

Niall reached into his bag and pulled out a couple of potion vials. He tossed one at his brother. "If its anything like last time, she'll come in hard and angry."

"Shouldn't we talk about this?" Erik shoved the vial into his front pocket.

"There is nothing to talk about. I've been told to take care of the wraith in the forest and that is what I'm going to do." Niall pushed forward, focusing his attention on his surroundings. The whistling became louder and the air colder.

"You're in love with Charlotte," Erik yelled.

Niall balled his hand into a fist. "The statue is this way."

"At least admit it to yourself, coward." Erik moved past him.

"I have." Niall's voice rose over the wind. "But that doesn't matter and it doesn't make it somehow better. Why would she ever want a man like me? After all we have done to her. After all I have done in my life. I don't deserve that kind of happily ever after. She'd be better off with Euann."

"Except Euann doesn't really love her. He just feels guilty about Helena." Erik had to shout to be heard over the wind. The whistle became a screech. "If any of us deserve happiness, it's ya, brother. We all know the sacrifices ya have made to protect this family. And, aye, we probably put too much of that responsibility on ya but ya never said ya don't want it. Ya never say ya want anything. So if ya want Charlotte," as Erik spoke the last words, the screeching stopped and he was left yelling in the silent forest, "get your hairy ass on over to her and tell her."

Both Niall and his brother looked around.

"She'd be lucky to have ya," Erik finished, sounding almost distracted. "Where did Helena go?"

"Hello, laddies, it's been a long while." A sweet voice came from before them on the path, not belonging to a body that he could see. The woman had a British accent.

"Did ya hear that?" Erik whispered.

Niall nodded and lifted a hand for silence. In the other, he clutched the potion vial and twisted the cork with his thumb and forefinger to loosen it. He listened to the forest, each rustle of leaves and stirring of branches. Erik's breathing buried some of the noise and made it harder to decipher where the spirit might be hiding.

Suddenly, Erik flew backward. His heels dragged on the ground as if he was being pushed by an unseen force. Niall howled as he ran after his brother to stop the attack. Erik stumbled, righting himself. A blast of cold air hit Niall and he turned to find a blue streak of light zipping down the path.

"Helena, stop," Niall ordered.

The blue light obeyed, the streak gathering together until it formed the ethereal shape of a woman. Helena turned. Her beauty was so much more than he remembered. She walked toward him like a seductress.

"Are you going to help me, Niall? Are you going to fix it? Are you going to give me my life back?" The words were soft and sweet, and incredibly deceptive. He felt the anger radiating off her even as she smiled. It seeped from her, prickling his warlock senses. As she neared, her eyes darkened into black pits and her voice deepened. "I didn't think so."

Niall didn't understand how Helena could be so lucid. She was no ordinary wraith, but then, she had not had an ordinary death. But if she could speak, maybe she could also listen. He didn't use the potion. "Helena, ya know we never meant to hurt ya."

"Would you take it all back if you could?" she asked.

"Aye." Niall nodded.

"Niall, careful," Erik warned.

"Would you rewind time?" she asked.

Niall started to nod, only to stop. He watched her suspiciously.

She leaned closer to whisper in his ear. "Would you let me see the truth if that meant I would look at you the way you see me every day?"

"What is she talking about?" Erik asked.

"How...?" Niall tensed. How could she have heard the words he'd meant for Charlotte?

He felt the cold press of lips to his cheek before Helena walked through him. She pulled at his power, using it as fuel for herself. "An amazing ripple of power washed over me, bad luck for the MacGregors meant good luck for me. It woke me up. Ley lines did the rest. Luck and ley lines, a convergence of happenstance."

"What do ya want, Helena? Do ya understand that ya are long dead? Nothing is as ya left it. Move on. Find peace." Erik held his vial a little more openly as he moved next to Niall.

"You stole from me," Helena said, staring at the brothers. "You took it all—my memories, my love, my sanity, and then my life. You even took my death, bringing me with you across the ocean to this place. You didn't even let me rest in the soil of my homeland. Those sins don't just go away. Those sins must be atoned for. There is a debt to be paid. That is when I'll find my peace."

"What do ya want? My atonement? I'm sorry, Helena." Niall put his hand on Erik's to stop him from lifting the vial.

"Ya can't trust her, Niall," Erik whispered. "She is no longer a woman. That is not innocence ya see in her face."

Helena laughed. "I will take from you, as you have from me. I will take your love and the memories you would have had, and in doing so I will take *your* sanity. After that, you will be as good as dead."

Niall and Erik lifted their potion vials at the same time, released the corks, and threw them at her feet. Smoke curled from the liquid but her laughter only grew. The magick did not affect her as it should have.

Instead, she gave a small shiver. "Oh, that tickles."

"Don't do this," Niall said.

"I would take it all back if I could," Helena said, looking sincere as she mocked the words he'd whispered to himself about Charlotte. "I would rewind time if it would fix the future. I would let ya see the truth if that meant ya would look at me once the way I see ya every day."

"What is she talking about?" Erik asked.

"Ya will not harm her," Niall growled, lunging at Helena. He shifted as he flew toward her, using the strength of the wolf and the power of the warlock to make her corporeal so he could push her against a tree.

"Thank the luck demon for me. I couldn't have done this without him," Helena said before dissipating into a mist. Niall's clawed hands sank into the bark as Helena fled.

Charlotte!

The one word focused in his mind as panic filled him. Helena would go after Charlotte.

Niall stayed shifted as he ran on all fours. His messenger bag dragged on the ground, forcing him onto two shifted legs. The wolf was faster than the man. He heard his brother running behind him and glanced back to see Erik shifted into panther form. The smell of ash greeted them as they neared the burnt goblin den marking the way to the back of the mansion.

When Niall would have run toward Lydia's house, Erik shifted into his human form and called, "Niall, the mirror!"

Niall switched routes, shifting from his wolf form to follow Erik inside. They hurried through the mansion, up the stairs.

"Niall? Erik?" Euann yelled as they passed. "What's happening?"

"Helena is loose," Erik said.

"Helena?" Euann started to run after them.

"Call Iain," Niall ordered. "Have him bring Jane. Everyone is to stay in this house."

Erik went to his room in the mansion where he kept a full-size portal mirror that would take them directly into the Victorian house he shared with Lydia. Dark wood accented the lightly colored walls of the room. A large painting of Erik in full MacGregor plaid similar to the one Niall had was set against the frame of the mirror. The canvas had been ripped down the middle. Erik grabbed it and thrust the painting aside before stepping into his own reflection.

Niall followed him into the mirror.

Chapter Fifteen

"Sounds like a storm is coming." Lydia stood and moved toward the kitchen window.

Charlotte felt a small panic wash over her. The light changed and she stood from the table. Blue lit up the kitchen from outside, flashing like a camera through all the windows.

Lydia didn't seem to notice. "Listen to that wind screech."

Charlotte felt the cold creeping in on her. She shook violently and balled her hands into her lap. The light flashed again as she stared out of the window and day turned into night. She'd been through enough hallucinations to know this couldn't be real. If she just held still maybe it would go away.

"*It's real. Magick is real.*" Charlotte gasped, turning to look toward the living room as she heard a recording of her voice. The pop and scratch of an old record player filled the silence between words. "*You said it was, but spells are one thing.*"

"*It's okay. We're safe in here,*" Lydia answered.

Charlotte looked at the window. Lydia was gone. Her voice came from the living room, answering Charlotte's memory.

"*Your house is glowing blue. Why is your house glowing blue?*" her recorded voice said, the words coming out of nowhere, like a haunting.

"*That's how I know we're safe,*" Lydia answered. "*It's Gramma's barrier spell. He can't get in unless I invite him.*"

"*Like a vampire.*" Charlotte heard the hysteria in her recorded voice, but felt the fear in her chest as if it was currently happening. Her heart physically ached each time it beat, sending a constricting pain over her lungs. "*Nothing is ever going to be normal again...*"

Another flash of blue lit up the windows, prompting Charlotte to stand from the table. This hallucination wasn't going away. She forced herself to confront the memory but as she reached the doorway, it was to see an image of herself on the couch with Lydia fading into noth-ingness.

Lightning flashed through the window, followed by the crack of thunder. Charlotte inched toward the couch to look out the big picture window. The storm picked up force, blowing leaves and sticks across the lawn. A plastic bag rolled toward the tree line.

"You don't have to stay, Charlotte. I'll under-stand if you want to go home." Lydia's recording was back, this time coming from the kitchen.

"I'm not leaving you," Charlotte answered. *"Gramma Annabelle? Are you here?"*

"I've been trying to talk to her all night. She won't appear, and I don't know how to make her," Lydia said. A series of crashes sounded as if the house was being torn apart. She saw curtains fly past the doorway to the kitchen. *"Let's try redeco-rating. Remodeling is supposed to stir spirits because it changes the environment."*

She saw movement in the shadows. The table slid across the floor, knocking the chairs aside. Charlotte gasped, jumping back. The voices were familiar, and the actions became more so, but then so was the intense fear growing with each moment.

Curtains were pulled off the windows behind

her. Furniture slid across the floor, pushed by unseen hands. Lotion bottles flew from the shelves, crashing all around her. Charlotte cried out and lifted her hands to protect her head. She closed her eyes tight, wanting the hallucination to go away. She didn't want to be crazy. She wanted to be normal.

Nothing is ever going to be normal again. The thought repeated itself in her mind, even as she tried to think past it.

Suddenly, the destruction stopped and Charlotte was left standing in a destroyed home. But outside, the pounding storm only became worse. She wasn't sure what to do. The hallucination didn't fade. Tears slid over her cheeks. She didn't want to be crazy. None of this could be real, but the pelt of lotion bottles as they'd struck her said differently.

Lightning flashed and Erik appeared in the curtain-less window. Charlotte yelped in surprise and jumped back. She pressed her hand against her chest. Storm clouds rolled and the room became darker. Erik's eyes glinted with light as his face shifted and changed. Fangs grew. Fur covered his features. He lifted a clawed hand and began tapping the glass.

Nothing is ever going to be normal again.

Charlotte took a deep breath. She'd been so terrified when she saw the shift, but felt that fear leaving her now. Niall was a werewolf, and as terrifying as he looked, he hadn't hurt her. Erik would not hurt Lydia. This was the past. Nothing was going to happen to her. She was safe. This was over.

Wind rattled the house, threatening to tear it apart. Trees cracked, thick limbs rolling over the yard. Leaves swirled like blizzard snow.

"I should have made you leave," Lydia said.

A loud thud sounded overhead and Charlotte looked up the stairs. Daylight returned to the windows. The memory was over.

"That'll be Erik," Lydia said, coming from the kitchen. She touched Charlotte's shoulder as she passed. She started up the stairs.

Charlotte looked around the living room. It was put back into order. Lydia didn't seem to notice what had happened.

She took a deep breath. The memories of that night were back. Some a little hazy, but there if she concentrated hard enough. Angus MacGregor had ordered his son to erase her mind because she had been terrified. When Niall took that night from her, he'd also taken her back from the edge of insanity.

Charlotte remembered the look on Niall's face as he'd come for her. He'd been so sad, so sorry. He'd keep that look from his family. At the time, she'd been so scared that she hadn't been able to comprehend what was happening to her.

"Lydia," Erik called.

"Here," Lydia answered on her way up the stairs.

"Is Charlotte still with ya?" Niall appeared on the stairwell, rushing down past Lydia. His panicked eyes met hers. He hurried to the kitchen, checking the house, before he rejoined them. "We need to go."

"Niall?" Charlotte asked in confusion.

"It's not safe," Erik insisted, taking Lydia's hand.

"Charlotte, it's all right. Come on." Lydia motioned that she should follow.

"What is going on?" Charlotte asked Niall as the other two went up the stairs. "Where did you come from? I didn't hear the door open."

"We need to get ya back to the mansion. There is a portal mirror in Lydia's room that will take us there." Niall hesitated before taking her hand. "Trust me. Please."

Charlotte felt the heat of his palm against hers and nodded. "I trust you."

At that, Niall smiled and nodded. He gestured for her to go up the stairs first, staying behind her as if to protect her from anything that might come. She went to Lydia's room. Upon entering, she gasped at seeing her friend disappear into the antique mirror one of Erik's relatives gave her as an engagement gift.

"It's safe. Like stepping across a threshold." Niall poked his hand through the glass, bringing it back unharmed.

"That is so cool," Charlotte said, to his obvious surprise. She went to the mirror and put her hand into her reflection. When it didn't hurt, she closed her eyes and stepped through. Her foot found firm footing inside the mirror and when she opened her eyes, she was in the MacGregor mansion. A torn painting of Erik indicated it must have been his bedroom. Lydia motioned for her to follow as she went through the door.

Niall stepped in behind her. "The family will be downstairs."

"Wait." Charlotte grabbed his arm. "I remembered the night Erik shifted and made that storm hit the house."

"I will explain, I promise, but—"

"Let me say this," she interrupted. "I know you did what you thought you had to. You weren't sure you could trust me and I was..."

"Broken," Niall supplied.

"That's one way to look at it," she said. "I know your father ordered you to take my memories. I know that you were worried I'd say something, or do something. I just wanted you to know that I understand why you did it."

"It wasn't just about the memories. I was trying to take your fear." Niall glanced at the door seconds before it opened.

Erik poked his head inside. "Niall, coming?"

Niall nodded. "We can talk about this later. Right now, there is another threat to our family."

"Our?" Charlotte tried to hide her smile. She liked the sound of that.

"Ya are like a sister to Lydia, that makes ya family," he explained.

Her pleasure lessened somewhat at his explanation. He guided her by the elbow toward the bedroom door.

Chapter Sixteen

"Helena is back." Erik's announcement hung over the silent room like a noose. The family gathered in the library, the one room that had been protected from invasion. Centuries of spells and residual magick radiated from the old books and herb jars to form a protective shield over the immediate area.

Euann and Rory sat on a couch. Cait stood behind them. Angus leaned against an oak desk next to where his wife sat behind it. Lydia motioned to Charlotte to sit next to her in an over-sized chair. The two women fit snuggly next to each other but neither seemed to mind.

"Where are the others?" Niall asked.

"Iain and Jane are on their way," Euann said with a worried glance at Charlotte.

"She'll be fine," Niall answered. "Won't ya?"

Charlotte nodded at his prompting.

"Murdoch is handling the water sprite migration," Cait said to explain her husband's absence. "I thought it best not to call him back."

"Agreed," Angus said. "Best to keep the sprites on course."

"Raibeart is, uh, indisposed," Euann said.

"What do ya mean?" Angus demanded. "What is more important than this?"

"He better not be running around naked, not tonight, not with a wraith threat," Cait added.

Rory began to laugh. "For some reason, Raibeart is convinced a giant chicken is roaming the woods, and he's dead set on having the biggest fried chicken ever known to man."

Niall cleared his throat.

"Oh, good gods," Margareta muttered in frustration. "And where is my daughter?" They glanced around the room at each other. "No one told Malina we were meeting?"

Niall watched as his family shook their heads in denial. "It's probably for the best. Dar is the reason Helena is so powerful right now. His dose of bad luck for the family boosted her consciousness enough to set her free."

"How do ya know it is Helena?" Angus asked his sons.

"Erik and I saw her," Niall said. "We went to the forest to track down the wraith like Cait ordered me to. We found Helena."

"She threatened us." Erik turned to Lydia and Charlotte. "She seeks revenge by hurting those we care about."

"No offense," Rory sat forward, placing his elbow on his knees, "but what does this have to do with Charlotte? If Helena wants to hurt the family, why would she go after Charlotte?"

"Gee, none taken," Charlotte mumbled under her breath.

Niall refused to look at her, not wanting to give their relationship away. Charlotte had made it clear she wanted to keep it a secret.

"Helena knows we are protecting Charlotte. She knows that she is important to the family," Erik answered.

Though his oldest brother knew better, Niall was grateful Erik didn't give away his secret. He didn't want to suffer teasing from his family if they found out he was in love with Charlotte, especially since she did not love him back.

"Helena said—" Charlotte began to speak, only

to stop. She lowered her eyes. "Sorry, I didn't mean to interrupt."

"What?" Margareta prompted.

"Helena took me to where she's trapped," Charlotte said. "Gramma Annabelle said something about slipping into me and trying to make me walk downtown to hide her spell bags. I'm guessing that's what Helena did. I saw her in the forest and the next thing I know, I'm waking up on a slab of stone in the forest. She said I couldn't trust you. If I did, I would end up like her, imprisoned in a statue."

"We would have seen this sooner if someone hadn't used my surveillance cameras for target practice," Euann muttered, glancing sideward at his cousin. "I had that entire area covered."

Rory looked guiltily away.

"Stop bickering," Cait ordered. She lifted her hand in warning. A yellow glow swirled around her fingertips as she threatened to petrify them. Rory and Euann looked properly scolded.

"We think she's coming for Charlotte first," Erik said.

Charlotte's eyes rounded. Niall would not have told her as bluntly as his brother, but she needed to know she was in danger.

Niall looked at her until she met his gaze. "We won't let anything happen. Ya are under the protection of this family."

"Aye," Angus agreed. "We have stood as caretakers for Helena long enough. It is time to end this."

"What happened to Helena?" Lydia asked. "I've heard the name mentioned, but I don't think anyone has told her story. I'm assuming she had her memories erased like Charlotte?"

"Not like Charlotte," Erik said.

"We were not as versed in the mind as we are now," Niall added.

"There is no story to tell," Margareta stated, stopping all explanation. "The past is the past. Today we fight and end this. It is what is best for all involved. There is no saving a soul once it succumbs to the rage of a wraith. All we can do is set it free."

"We tried reasoning with her." Niall wanted this to be over. He wanted Charlotte safe. He wanted to hop on his motorcycle and ride away from Green Vallis until he forgot what she looked like. He wanted to rid himself of the hold she had over him.

"If she is strong enough to threaten us, then she

is aware enough for us to catch her." Cait moved to the shelf and began tapping her finger along the spines of the books she found there. "I believe there is an amulet that might help."

"The wraith potion did not affect her," Erik said.

"Maybe ya missed," Euann said. "Are ya sure ya hit her with it?"

"We did not miss," Niall said in irritation. "She was hit with it twice and merely laughed."

"Cait," Margareta stated.

"Aye, we'll make a stronger batch," Cait answered. The two women had known each other long enough to be able to fill in the blanks of their short discussion.

"We'll work through the night," Margareta said.

"What about Dar?" Charlotte asked. "If he gave her good luck, can he just give her bad, too?"

"Too unpredictable." Niall shook his head. "She's awake now. There is no telling what luck would do to her."

"Bad luck for a wraith could affect a lot of innocent people. Those things have a way of spreading." Margareta joined Cait by the bookshelf, taking a volume and opening it.

"What if she comes tonight?" Charlotte asked.

"Ya will be safe as long as ya are in the house," Angus assured her. "Euann, will ya stay with Char—"

"I'll keep Charlotte with me. I won't sleep tonight. She can have my bed." Niall was not about to let his brother stay with Charlotte for the night. He wanted to make sure she was safe.

Erik suppressed a grin. Euann wrinkled his brow while Rory whispered something in his ear.

"Perhaps that is best," his da agreed. "Ya have dealt with this wraith before."

Chapter Seventeen

Charlotte looked over the carpet picnic set up in Niall's bedroom. Since the family focused their magick on repairing the home, they had yet to materialize furniture and there was no dining room table downstairs. The idea that someone could simply will a dining set into existence was incredible to think about.

Instead of asking her what she might like, Niall brought a variety of food. There was a bowl of pasta, deli meats and cheeses to make sandwiches, chips and dip, and a bottle of whiskey. Euann had insisted on ordering pizzas, so a tray of different slices was also provided. Despite the circumstances, it was actually quite romantic. All that was missing was candlelight and a date who didn't pace in front of the window looking for trouble.

"So, I have a question." Charlotte eyed Niall's back.

"Only one? I would assume ya have many," Niall answered, still looking out over the evening landscape.

"Fine, I have many questions," Charlotte acknowledged with a small laugh. "When you said you got me a new king-size bed, did you buy me a bed? Or did you will it into existence with a two-second spell?"

Niall chuckled. "Actually, I had it delivered. Malina has the gift for materializing. My talents lay in other areas."

"Why don't you come away from that window?" Charlotte patted the floor next to her, indicating that he should join her. "Your family seems to think I'll be safe in here. Besides, there's enough food for the both of us and an army."

Niall studied her for a long moment before finally joining her. His kilt covered his thighs, but left enough of his legs exposed to make her view interesting. He made sure to keep his distance and sat across from her, keeping the food between them.

Charlotte wondered at that but didn't ask him to move closer. "That's probably a good call, sitting over there. I do have a tendency to bite."

"It's not your bite I'm worried about, love." He leaned over and pinched a tortilla chip between his thumb and forefinger. As he lifted it to his lips, the gesture was more seductive than it should have been. She found herself staring at his mouth and licking her own lips.

The way he looked at her gave the impression he knew exactly the effect he had on her. How could he not? Whenever he was near, her breathing deepened and she had to tell herself not to stare too long. Knowing they had been intimate, knowing she wanted to do it again, left her trembling and excited. She knew he wanted her. Charlotte liked to think a woman instinctively understood those kinds of things when it came to a man's attention and affection. It may have taken her a while to realize it, but then again, she had been mentally unwell, so it's no wonder she missed the chemistry flowing between them.

"What is your next question?" His voice sounded gruff but she had come to realize that was just his way. Niall was not one for small talk. He kept his emotions hidden and thoughts to himself.

Charlotte eyed the chips, wondering if his lips would taste salty if she leaned over to kiss him. The first time he'd brought her food, he'd picked up all her favorites. "What is your favorite food?"

"No one has ever asked me that." He hummed thoughtfully. "Funnel cake with powdered sugar."

At that, she arched a brow and laughed. She picked up a piece of cheese and nibbled on it. "That's not real food."

"Says who?" he defended.

"Every mother ever," Charlotte argued. "What is your second favorite food?"

"Giant corndogs in sweet ketchup." He ate another chip, not even pausing to think as he answered.

"Third?"

"Funnel cake with strawberries."

"Fourth?" This was just getting sad.

"Beer-battered cheese curds."

"Fifth?"

"Giant turkey legs."

"Sixth?" At this point, she kept asking just to hear his answers.

"Vanilla ice cream shake."

"Do you like anything that doesn't come from the county fair?"

He shrugged. "I like fairs."

Niall clearly wasn't one for elaborating without a little prodding.

"I never would have guessed you for a fair guy." She looked over his rugged demeanor. "I would have guessed biker bar, or a motorcycle club, but not a—"

"Ya think I'm just some thug." He took a napkin and wiped the chip dust from his fingers.

"No."

"Just a slumlord then."

"I shouldn't have said that. I was angry. I hadn't been sleeping, and the water kept leaking on me, and I thought you didn't care. I was wrong. Please accept my apology for that."

He nodded. "Accepted."

"So why do you like fairs?" She reached for a slice of beef and mushroom pizza.

"What's not to like? The unusual vegetable competition, the pie-eating contests, butter sculptures," Niall paused, as he lifted the whiskey bottle, "kids having a good time without a care in the world, men trying to impress their girlfriends by winning stuffed bears, and the funnel cakes."

"You are a lot more than you seem, Niall MacGregor." Charlotte set down her half-eaten slice of pizza and held her hand out to take the whiskey bottle. She opened it and took a small drink. The liquor burned and she gave a light cough before handing it back.

"And ya are not half as crazy as everyone believed, Charlotte Carver," he teased.

Charlotte laughed. "You're nothing like I expected."

He started to speak but then lifted the bottle, cutting off his own words.

She took a deep breath and let it out slowly. "I can't explain how wonderful it feels to remember things again. To feel like my mind is not running away from me."

"Ya have not had the easiest go of it." He took another drink.

"Neither have you." She held out her hand to take the bottle from him and set it on the floor, out of his reach.

"What makes ya say that?"

"I see it in your eyes. I feel it when I'm close to you. There is so much inside you, so much that is buried deep and kept restrained." Charlotte stood. "I'm going to say this and hope that it makes sense to you. I have all these strange memories swimming around in my head. I know they're real. I know they scared me. I can feel every other emotion, but I know that you took that fear from me. It's because of you that I can face what happened. So, I guess my next question, Niall, is what happened to that fear? I see your face when I close my eyes. I hear you whispering in my dreams, but I can't hear what you say. Or if I do hear it, I can't remember when I wake up. You're always there, even when you weren't."

He didn't speak.

She held out her hand to him. "I like you. I like being with you. I feel safe when I'm with you."

"Charlotte, what you're feeling is—"

"I have never been clearer in my life. And trust me when I say that coming from me, that says a lot. I know what it's like to not know my own mind. I know myself better than I ever have. I know what I want. And right now, I want you to stand up, walk over here, and kiss me."

Niall examined the tips of his fingers as if contemplating her words. He nodded slowly. He lifted his hand, turning off the lights. Seconds later, the fire blazed in the fireplace.

Pushing his fist against the floor, he stood. His eyes met hers, full of determination. He moved with a predatory grace around the picnic to come before her. He was a man of few words but in this instance, he didn't need them.

His hand lifted to cup her cheek. Niall pulled her face toward his, claiming her mouth. His tongue slipped between her lips, delving deep as he lay claim. There was no mistaking when he kissed her that he wanted to. And he wanted more.

The animal inside him glinted in his eyes. Everything about him was primitive and raw. He kissed with aggression, letting her feel how much he wanted her. His hands moved over her as if trying to devour her with his fingers. He tugged at her clothes and, when they did not come off, he pulled his mouth away. He gestured his hand and made them magically melt from her body onto the floor.

Niall pulled his shirt over his head. His eyes roamed her naked body freely. He walked her back toward the bed, not touching her as he unfastened his kilt. Scars lined his strong body, a testament to his dangerous life. He pushed his kilt down, letting it land at his feet.

Charlotte's legs hit the mattress and she crawled onto the bed. He reached behind her knees and pulled her back toward the edge of the bed. He stood over her, letting her legs dangle next to his hips. She felt the beast within him and wanted to tame it. He took his time looking at her. He ran his hands up her stomach only to stop when he reached her breasts. His fingers teased the hard peaks. She wiggled beneath him, inching her hips to the edge of the bed.

Being with Niall was unlike anything she had ever experienced. He was forceful and gentle at the same time.

He held her by her legs and delved forward. When his body joined with hers, it created a perfect rhythm. She watched his muscles move with each thrust. The pleasure built until it was too much. They came in unison. Charlotte gasped, crying out softly. He stiffened, leaning his head back as his lips parted in a silent howl.

Afterward, he moved to lie next to her on the bed. He stroked the hair from her face. His gaze moved as if he memorized every nuance of her.

Charlotte suppressed a yawn. She skated her fingers over his chest, moving from scar to scar. "I want to help tomorrow, with Helena. For whatever reason, she reached out to me. I think I can help."

"No."

"Just no?" Charlotte dropped her hand and leaned back to give him her sternest expression.

"Helena is not what ya think. She's not some woman ya can reason with. She's from a different time." Niall placed his hand on hers, keeping it against his chest as he rolled onto his back.

"What happened? Why is she so mad?"

"It doesn't matter. It's in the past. We have to think about tomorrow. There is much to be done. We should sleep." He closed his eyes and lifted a finger. The curtains pulled shut, hiding them from the outside world—not that anyone could see them on the second floor of the mansion.

Well, scratch that. No one who wasn't a flying supernatural trying to peek inside windows.

His breathing became even. She couldn't tell if he really slept or if he faked it. Charlotte held her eyes open for as long as she could, watching to see if he peeked at her. He did not. And as her lids became heavy, she let the gentle lull of sleep overtake her.

Chapter Eighteen

"Oh, what the fuck is happening now?" Charlotte muttered to herself.

The countryside wasn't something she recalled from her past. Besides the fact it didn't look gloomy and some invisible record didn't pop and scratch to distort sound, she was pretty sure she had never been to a place that had a castle in the background.

A woman screamed and Charlotte jumped in fright. She searched the surrounding meadow. The grasses parted as if some invisible force ran past her.

"Char, don't follow the ghost," she tried to command herself. She closed her eyes. "Don't do it. Just stay here until you're back in Niall's bed."

"Helena, wait," Euann said. His accent was a little thicker, but she recognized his voice.

"Stay away from me, Euann MacGregor! I saw what your brother is. He is in league with the devil! If you don't help me, you are in league yourself and the MacGregor witches must be stopped," a British-accented woman answered. Was that Helena? She hardly sounded like the ghost Charlotte had met by the statue.

Charlotte saw the grass part but there were no people walking through it. The sound of hooves beat on the ground. She turned to see a black horse charging at her. The creature ran right through her.

Helena screamed again. Her figure came into view, running away from the horse. She wore a gown that looked like it belonged in the eighteenth century. The heavy skirts weighed her steps, even as she lifted them to run.

Charlotte turned her attention to the horse rider. His hair was much longer but she would recognize that kilt anywhere. Niall chased Helena.

Charlotte found herself running after them. Euann appeared in the grasses next to her, a younger version than the man she knew. He did not acknowledge that he saw her running around in a memory that was not hers to explore.

As they ran, the landscape changed. Euann disappeared, turning into a tree. They were near some ruins, the stone walls giving shelter as Niall knelt on the ground next to Helena.

"Och, I am sorry, lassie," Niall whispered. "I wish ya would not have seen what ya did, but your grannie was an evil woman. She summoned the beast that devoured her. I did not make it in time to save her."

Helena didn't answer. The wind blew, stirring Niall's clothes, but Helena kept perfectly still.

"It won't hurt, I promise. Ya can go on as ya have." Niall lifted his hands over Helena. "I have to protect the family. There are those who would see the witch trials brought back in a blink of an eye. We have already lost far too many."

Charlotte walked around the campsite. Niall's eyes lightened in color as he whispered an incantation. Tiny sparks moved from Helena's face toward his hands. The sparks grew, showing the faintest hint of a figure screaming before bursting and falling to the ground like spent ash. This must have been how they erased memories.

"Please forgive me," Niall whispered to himself as he plucked Helena's memories.

"Niall, stop!" Iain ran from the darkness.

"Da said we have to," Niall said. "It is my mess and I have to clean it up. She threatens to expose the entire family."

"Ma said stop. Her bloodline is too strong. When her grannie died the powers would have passed on. It's too dangerous," Iain insisted. "We don't know what will happen if we take the memory of a witch. She's not like other humans now."

Niall stopped and dropped his hands. "It's too late. I already took them."

Iain looked worried. "Did ya get them all?"

"I don't know, I think?" Niall looked helpless.

"We have to go. The family leaves England tonight. They sent me to bring ya back." Iain pulled at Niall's arm.

"What should we do about her?" Niall hesitated.

"Leave her. By the time she thaws, we'll be gone." Iain threw up his arms. "I've put a spell on this place. No one will find her before she wakes up. She'll be fine."

Niall nodded. Iain ran back the way he came.

Niall took a deep breath. "Choose a better path than your grannie." He ran after his brother.

Charlotte opened her eyes, finding herself next

to Niall's naked body. Firelight still danced over him. He made a strange noise in his sleep as if haunted by the past.

She tapped his chest. "Niall, wake up."

Instantly, he stiffened and moved as if to look around. "What is it? Does Helena come?"

"I think I was in your head again," she said. "I saw these ruins and you were taking memories out of Helena. I could see you didn't want to. Then Iain came and..."

"Ya saw that?" Niall sat up and placed his hands on his head. "I can't explain why this is happening. Ya shouldn't be in my head."

"Why not? You were in mine." Charlotte ran her hand over his naked back, trying to give him comfort. "I don't know why you're so upset. I saw what happened. She was going to turn you in to the authorities and hurt your family. I don't know a ton about the witch trials, but I've seen enough documentaries to know I would do anything to protect my loved ones from such a fate."

"I made a mistake that night," Niall said. "I wish I could go back and change it, but..."

His words sparked a memory and she tried to hold on to it.

I would take it all back if I could. I would

rewind time if it would fix the future. I would let ya see the truth if that meant ya would look...

The rest of the words were lost.

"Come here." She pulled him into her arms, forcing him to lie down. "Tell me."

"Helena saw me," he said.

"Saw you what?"

"Her grandmother was a powerful woman. She summoned a demon to do her bidding. I was so young, only about a hundred years old, and I had never fought anything so powerful. The demon turned on the old witch the first moment it could, as demons do, and I was too late to save her. Helena had this horrible crush on Euann. He flirted with her but it never went anywhere. She used to sneak out of her grandmother's house, and on this particular night, coming home, she saw me with the demon, then saw her grandmother was dead, so she thought I sent the beast."

Charlotte stroked his hair from his brow. "Go on."

"Helena could not be reasoned with. Euann tried." Niall closed his eyes. "My da decided since she saw me, I would be the best one to find the memories and erase them. However, my ma and Aunt Cait traced Helena's bloodline, realized the power she inherited, and sent Iain to stop me. It was too late. I'd left a gap in Helena's memory, and her powers filled it with lies and insanity. I'd missed one memory of that night and her powers created this fantastical tale of what had gone on. She came after us, started doing these really odd, bad things. She walked backward for a day and told everyone witches made her with a curse. She painted nonsense symbols on the side of a barn with chicken blood. Then she began accusing others of witchcraft—innocent people she didn't like the look of. The old timers believed her."

Charlotte nodded, keeping quiet as he spoke. The even drawl of his accent was soft.

"Helena started writing these spells, old spells no one had thought of for a long time. Her power just kept filling in blanks, and since it had spent centuries being tainted with dark magick, that is where it took her. Because she knew I had been there the night her grandmother died, she focused on my family. We tried to stop her. We managed to take more of the memories, but by then the damage had been done. She'd written things down, and as she read her letters to herself, her powers became even more distorted, until finally anger changed the young girl she had been. We wanted to help her, but couldn't. She was too powerful, and too unstable."

"So you trapped her in stone?" Charlotte asked.

"Aye. First, we stripped her of her magick. With her being the last of her bloodline, the inherited powers dissipated into the world. What was left of her, we put into a hollow in the statue. We had hoped time would show us a way to help her."

"And so your family has been protecting her statue ever since?"

"Every move we make, she comes with us."

"And now she's out and seeking revenge." Charlotte shivered.

"I won't let her hurt ya, Charlotte." Niall pulled her against his chest. "I promise. I will not fail ya."

Charlotte believed him. Still, tears threatened her eyes and she turned in his arms to place her back against his chest to hide them. It became very clear now. His protectiveness was his way of atoning for what happened to Helena. He cared for her, but he did not love her. Not as she loved him.

The pain was almost unbearable, but she couldn't bring herself to leave his embrace. If just for tonight, she would pretend this moment meant as much to him as it did to her.

"You did all you could for her, and for me," Charlotte whispered. "None of this is your fault. You couldn't have known what would happen to Helena when you tried to save your family. I know you tried to save her, just as you saved me. You have nothing to be sorry for. You need to forgive yourself. You also will not face her alone. If you could have defeated her on your own, you would have. She needs me. I'm not sure why but she does. Tomorrow, I will go with you."

He didn't answer, and she had no idea if he heard her.

Chapter Nineteen

Charlotte felt a soft caress against her cheek and smiled. Sleeping next to Niall made her feel safe. She felt rested as if her mind finally went into that deep place of normal dreams.

She stretched her arm, reaching for him. Instead of a naked hip, her hand glided over soft material.

Charlotte frowned, if Niall wasn't in bed with her, who was touching her face?

Another feathery caress brushed her as light as a butterfly. Charlotte gasped, her body flailing as she swatted at her face.

It took a few moments to recognize Margareta MacGregor sitting on the edge of the bed. What was Niall's mother doing in the bedroom? Where was Niall?

Margareta held a scrap of red silk in her hand. Charlotte blinked, wondering if this was another memory. Swatches of material had fallen around her when she sat up. She touched her face and hair, pulling a few more pieces of silk from her locks.

"That red is," Margareta eyed Charlotte's hair, "interesting. It's very hard to match."

Charlotte touched the silk pieces on her lap, realizing she wore a man's T-shirt and a pair of sweatpants. Niall must have magickally dressed her. That was one trick she wouldn't mind having —dressing with a point of a finger, lighting fires, locking doors, cleaning. Why was Niall's mother placing color swatches on her? She handed the material strips back to the woman. "What is going on? Where's Niall?"

"Ya will make a lovely..." Margareta paused. "Are ya attached to that color? It is a difficult shade."

"Not really. I bought a box of it from the grocery store. I'm sure I can buy another and it will match just fine." Charlotte didn't mind the red and figured it would fade out eventually.

"I meant for dresses," Margareta said. She took

the silk and turned to lift a giant binder from the bed. It was overstuffed with pages, color swatches hanging over the sides. She stuffed the swatches into folder pocket. "I wanted to speak to ya before my daughters had a chance to put any ideas into your head."

"Daughters? Niall has more sisters? I thought it was only Malina."

"Lydia and Jane." Margareta flipped a few pages, stopping when she found a sketch of a horse-drawn carriage with doves. She held it up as if to gauge Charlotte's reaction. "And now ya will be joining us."

"And now I will...?" Charlotte repeated, stunned.

Margareta smiled, nodding her head toward the page. Horses, doves, was this a wedding planner?

"Oh, you're old-fashioned," Charlotte said, realizing what was happening. If Niall was several hundred years old, then Margareta would be...well, from a very different time. "No, no, I think you have the wrong idea. Niall and I aren't...we're just..." Charlotte tried to think of a delicate way to explain what they were. "Friends."

"Of course, friendship is important in

marriage." Margareta reached forward and patted her leg. "Ya are very smart to realize that. True love will only get ya through so many centuries."

"Centuries?" Charlotte's heart started to pound. "I have to ask you something."

"Anything," Margareta grinned, "daughter."

"Am I crazy? Did I lose time again?"

"Excuse me?" Margareta frowned in confusion.

Maybe it wasn't the next day like she thought. Maybe Niall didn't dress her in the T-shirt. "Did you all dig around in my brain and take more memories? Did something go wrong with Helena? Did something happen to me?"

The door opened and Lydia pushed her way inside. She wore the same jeans and T-shirt she had on the day before. "Ah-ha! Ma, we knew we'd find you in here."

"Seriously, Ma, what are you doing? Leave poor Charlotte alone." Malina followed Lydia into the bedroom. Her designer clothes were pristine, giving the impression she was about to step out of the mansion and onto a New York fashion runway. Large earrings, a chunky necklace, and heels completed the look.

"Hey, Charlotte, good to see you again. Sorry for the intrusion." Jane was slower to enter. Her curly brown hair was pulled to the top of her head to create a messy bun. She was dressed athletic and outdoorsy in yoga pants, a T-shirt, and running shoes, it suited the fact she owned the local nursery.

"Hey, Jane, it's fine," Charlotte answered. She looked at Lydia, trying to silently ask her best friend what was going on.

"Good, we're all here," Margareta said. "There is so much planning to do. The estate needs to be repaired. Malina, can ya see to Charlotte's hair?"

"I like her hair," Malina said.

"It won't match," Margareta insisted.

Malina shrugged and walked over toward the bed. She sat next to Charlotte.

"Ma, I thought we talked about this." Lydia sat down by Charlotte's feet. "Ya can't go around assuming people are going to get married."

Jane, who had always kept to herself, was slower to join them. She stood by the end of the bed.

"Niall is my baby boy. I think I'd know when my son has found a woman." Margareta went back to looking at her binder. "I could tell by the way he looked at her at yesterday's meeting."

"Ugh, put that hideous book away." Malina

waved her hand, sending the binder flying through the air.

Margareta countered the gesture with one of her own, ordering the book back onto the bed before it even hit the floor. "Do as you're told."

Malina huffed but touched Charlotte's hair. She combed her fingers through it, working her way up to the scalp. Charlotte could hear her muttering under her breath but didn't understand the words. She tried to pull away as her scalp began to tingle.

"Happy?" Malina asked her mother.

"It looks good," Jane told Charlotte.

"She always looks pretty," Lydia said.

"What is that on your finger?" Margareta demanded, pointing at Malina.

Malina held out her hand, showing a tattooed swirl around her ring finger. "You said Dar and I should have wedding rings. How do you like it?"

"This is what I get for sending ya to live with the English when ya were a babe," Margareta sighed.

"What about number sixty-three for Niall, Ma?" Malina asked with a small grin.

Charlotte arched a brow, seeing that Malina was changing the subject at her brother's expense.

She pushed up from the bed to look in the mirror by the dresser. Malina's magick had stripped the red from her hair, turning it back to her natural shade of brown. There was a shine to the waves as if she'd just left a salon. It was pretty, she'd give Malina that much.

"Sixty-three?" Margareta said thoughtfully, as she turned to the book. "Oh, the cherub choir shooting a bridge of arrows as the bride and groom float on a magickal cloud of...wait, no. This will never do for Niall. He wouldn't wear a silk loincloth. What about a rustic theme? Garlands of flowers hanging from the trees as the couple walks down a gemstone path to the sound of violins and flutes. Fairy lights everywhere and..."

Charlotte desperately grabbed Lydia by the arm. "Make this stop."

Lydia nodded. "Ma, I don't think Niall and Charlotte are engaged."

"But?" Margareta looked at Charlotte for confirmation.

"We're not even boyfriend and girlfriend." Charlotte tried to keep a neutral expression. She wanted there to be more between her and Niall than friendship, but she did not want his mother suspecting as much.

"But..." She motioned to the bed.

"All right, Ma, come on." Malina motioned that her mother should follow. "Bring your book. Let me tell you a little something about how boys and girls work in the modern age."

"I don't understand my children. I thought Niall would have at least asked her before going into battle with Helena." Margareta let her daughter lead her out of the room.

"Don't worry." Malina's voice became softer as she led her mother away. "I promise when it comes time for Euann to marry, I'll make sure he wears the silk cherub diaper and you can have as many spellbound doves as your heart desires."

"What the hell just happened?" Charlotte asked, looking at Lydia and Jane.

"You got MacGregored," Jane said with a small laugh.

"Omigod, so you have to spill," Lydia demanded. "What is going on with you and Niall?"

"Sex," Charlotte answered bluntly.

Jane gave a laugh of surprise and quickly covered her mouth to contain it.

"Please tell me Margareta is the crazy one today, not me," Charlotte said. "I woke up thinking I had lost time again."

"How should we put it?" Jane asked Lydia.

"She's the epitome of the stereotypical mother wanting to marry off her sons so that she can get grandchildren," Lydia said. "Then again, she's been waiting for hundreds of years."

"Should someone explain that you don't have to be married to—?" Charlotte started to ask.

"No," Lydia and Jane answered in unison.

"You do not want a Margareta MacGregor sex talk," Lydia said. "And don't mention being on birth control."

"Anyone else think it's strange that the MacGregors move here and suddenly, after waiting so long, all of them are suddenly getting married?" Charlotte looked around for a pair of shoes and found her boots tucked under the edge of the bed. She pulled them on, not caring that her outfit was a definite fashion don't. It's not like anyone would let her go home to get her own clothes. "I mean, what are the odds that the rest of them will find someone after all these years? You two were lucky."

"I don't think it's luck," Jane said. "I asked Iain about it. He said this town is special. It lies on a powerful convergence of energy that gives fuel to the supernatural. That's why the family was attracted to this place. It's also why other paranormal creatures are drawn here. I think it's why I stayed. The second I drove into town, it felt like home."

"Wait, so are you saying you're...?" Charlotte looked at Lydia.

"My mother was a *bean nighe*, which makes me half," Jane said.

"What's a *bean nighe*?" Charlotte asked.

"Banshee," Lydia said.

"Don't be scared. I'm not some screaming death omen, or anything. I'm more of a power conduit for warlocks, and I have a way with plants." Jane crossed to the window and pulled back the curtains. "Here, watch."

Charlotte moved to look out the window. Jane pressed her hands to the glass and closed her eyes. Charlotte watched over the treetops stretching in the distance against the dawn.

"I don't see anything," Charlotte said. "What am I looking for?"

Suddenly, vines crept over the glass from below, growing impossibly fast to cover the entire window. Jane lowered her hand.

"That's freaking cool!" Charlotte exclaimed.

Jane chuckled. "I'm still learning how to control it, but I have to say it's been great for business. No more losing nursery inventory, and it comes in helpful when I can ripen tomatoes for the farmers' market faster than before. Small-town businesses are hard enough to make flourish."

"So that's how you got all those extra fresh herbs at work," Charlotte said to Lydia.

"Jane lets me pay her in lotions and teas," Lydia explained.

Charlotte leaned against the window, peeking through the vines. Her expression fell as she thought about the statue hidden in the woods. "When do we go after Helena?"

"What do you mean?" Lydia asked.

"Helena, in the forest. When do we go?" Charlotte looked at them expectantly.

"Niall, Iain, Erik, and Euann left this morning," Jane said. "We're supposed to stay inside. Helena wants to hurt their women. We're safer here."

"I'm not staying behind," Charlotte countered. "I have to go with them. The bitch threatened me. She brought me out to her statue and said we were the same. I'm not going to hide while someone else goes and deals with it."

"Don't be stupid," Lydia said. "It's not some schoolyard bully they're up against. You'll only be in the way and make it harder for them. They'll be in more danger if they're focused on protecting you. I know you're worried, we all are—"

"I have to." Charlotte couldn't explain why, but she was compelled to fight. She'd seen inside Niall, and that gave her a strong feeling of what she needed to do.

"Please, Charlotte, don't," Jane said, trying to stop Charlotte from leaving the bedroom. She followed her into the hall. "Iain is out there."

Charlotte frowned, not following.

"What Jane means is that when we were attacked, you pulled Iain's powers. You both have been a little unsteady around each other since," Lydia explained.

"I can't stay here." What Charlotte *wasn't* saying is that she didn't want Niall fighting her battles for her. She wanted to prove she didn't need to be protected or lied to like some delicate flower they had to keep erasing. Sure, it might be stupid, but she needed to prove herself—to the MacGregors, to Niall, but mostly to herself. But that was only a small, selfish part of it. Seeing Jane's worry, she said, "I promise, I'll stay away from Iain. If I feel anything is amiss, I promise I'll run in the other direction from him."

Charlotte found Angus waiting at the bottom of the stairs. "I had a feeling ya would be coming down soon. It's good to see ya know to follow your intuition." He held out his hand, showing her a small bottle resting on his palm. "Ya will need this."

"What is it for?" Charlotte hesitated before she took it. Then leaning forward, she whispered, "Do you know what I'm supposed to do once I get there?"

"When the time is right, and the battle lost, drink it. I can feel my son's magick in ya. Follow your feelings." Angus stepped out of her way. "Ya might want to run. I can hear the screams."

Charlotte didn't understand, but found herself running for the garden door.

"And welcome to the family, lassie," Angus yelled behind her.

Chapter Twenty

Niall knew the wraith was toying with them. Her wailing screams came from all directions. It started just after dawn. He'd walked out of the house with his brothers, potion vials still warm in their hands from the cauldron. Cait had insisted they wear amulets of black obsidian for protection. The stones were supposed to help in the breaking of curses and ridding them of spirits who had become attached.

"Let me fly up and see if I can find her," Iain suggested, trying as the screams came from yet another direction. He was able to shift into various birds of prey. But, like Niall, the wildness of their shifted selves could be hard to control. It wasn't easy for Iain to know he could fly high above everything, wild and free. The right catalyst would keep him from transforming back into his human self.

"No," Niall said, his tone not leaving any room for argument. "Ya will be too exposed. She's too powerful. One gust and she could kill ya."

"We have to do something." Euann came from behind the statue of Helena.

Niall had noticed Euann wasn't meeting his gaze. It was also obvious that his family suspected there was much more going on between Niall and Charlotte than he was telling them.

"It's cracked near her heart." Euann motioned to Helena's likeness. "That is where she escaped."

"It doesn't matter how she got out, the fact is she's here and she's pissed," Erik said.

"Maybe we should take these off." Niall reached inside the neckline of his shirt and pulled out the amulet.

"Cait said not to." Euann lifted his potion bottle. "They're meant to protect us from the dark energy."

"Maybe they are doing too good a job," Iain said, agreeing with Niall.

"Leave the amulets on for now." Erik leaned over and reached into the duffel bag he'd brought with him. He pulled out a large clear container of salt. He tossed it at Euann. "Draw a circle around the area, make it thick, but leave an opening. If we can get her to come to us, we might be able to trap her inside."

"Aye," Euann agreed, doing as Erik requested.

The wailing continued. Niall reached for his neck. Without waiting for permission, he jerked the chain holding the protection stone. The necklace broke and he tossed it toward Iain when the other two weren't looking. His brother nodded at him and shoved it into his pocket.

The screaming stopped.

"Where is she?" Euann asked looking around.

Niall used his shifter hearing to listen to the wind. The sound of footsteps on the path caught his attention. A wraith would not be running.

"Crap," Niall swore.

"What?" Iain and Euann asked in unison.

"Who's out there?" Erik asked.

"Charlotte." Niall knew the answer even before he saw her. The sound of her running was like a signature. He knew everything about her.

"What is she doing out here?" Euann demanded.

Tension rolled over Niall and his brothers.

"Erik, I have held my tongue," Euann insisted.

"Ya told me Niall would protect her if I backed off my suit. This is not protection. We have to get her out of here."

"Euann, guilt is not love," Erik said. "No matter how many times ya say ya love the lassie does not make it true. Ya do not love Charlotte, not in the way ya should."

"He's right, brother," Iain added. "Every woman deserves a man who loves them fully."

"It is our fault she's damaged. She needs to be protected," Euann said. "She can't be out here. Not with Helena out of her prison."

Niall did not answer his brothers.

Niall's senses prickled in warning. Euann was right. Charlotte should not be in the forest. It was too dangerous. He went to the path and watched for Charlotte. He listened to her heavy breathing.

She came into view. Her steps slowed. "Niall—"

Helena flew from the trees, cutting off her words. She slammed into Charlotte, dragging her off the path into the trees.

Niall growled, shifting to run after them.

The darkness in Helena radiated from her, and he tracked them through the underbrush. He heard a thud and then running.

"Niall!" Charlotte cried out.

He ran toward her voice. He found her bent over on the forest floor.

"What the hell do ya think ya are doing?" The sound of his words was gruff as he came out of his shifted form, and barely understandable. He ran to her and pulled her into his embrace. His clothes had fallen off when he shifted and he didn't bother to materialize them back on.

Charlotte lifted her hand to show him a potion bottle. "I'm here to help. Angus told me to use this."

"Ya need to be back at the house where it is safe," he ordered. "He should not have let ya leave."

"She's after *me*. I need to be out here with you." Her eyes met his and they begged him to trust her.

"We need to lure her to the statue." Niall pointed in the direction of his brothers.

Charlotte gave a slight smile at his instruction and nodded.

Helena flew down from the trees. Niall jumped in front of her. He braced his feet as the wraith slammed into him.

Charlotte took off into the trees, running the

way he'd indicated. He tried to hold on to Helena. She lifted him off the ground. His feet swung as he tried to find footing. Suddenly, her body lost its corporeal form and he fell.

Niall landed on all fours. Pain shot up his wrists and ankles. He didn't care as he leapt forward to chase after Charlotte. He saw her running and darted to join her.

Niall materialized a kilt on his waist to protect him from the whip of low branches. He swept his arm around her, lifting her over his shoulder as he covered ground faster. Erik came from the forest and joined them in panther form, running behind Niall.

Euann held the container of salt near the opening he'd left in the circle. Niall dug in his heels, stopping before they crashed into the statue. He dropped Charlotte to her feet. Her breathing was still hard and fast from the run, but he swore she gave him a small smile. Her eyes gleamed as the adrenaline pumped through her veins.

Niall resisted the urge to shift, and stood next to her as a man.

"You sure do know how to show a girl a good time," Charlotte said. "If this weren't so important, I'd be enjoying myself."

Erik jumped into the salt circle. Helena chased him. She swooped down, flying to the side as she hit the barrier. She found the opening near Euann and came for Charlotte. Euann dumped the salt to complete the circle. Charlotte ducked. Helena hit the barrier and flew the other way, bouncing over them as she tried to break free. Niall pulled Charlotte close, holding her against him.

"Get out of the circle," Euann yelled. He stood on the other side of the salt barrier.

Erik and Iain jumped out. Niall tried to lift Charlotte with him but Helena appeared, blocking them. The wraith appeared calm. Charlotte's breathing was the only sound in the forest.

"They will only hurt you," Helena said. "Break you down. That is what the devil does. Tricks you with sweet smiles."

"No one wanted to hurt you," Charlotte said. "They tried to help. They did not call the demon that night to hurt your grandmother."

"How does she know that?" Euann asked. Niall ignored his brother.

"Helena, it is time for ya to move on," Niall commanded, trying to draw Helena's attention from Charlotte. He saw his brothers walking around the circle.

"You're right. It *is* time I moved on." Helena became a blur as she ran at Charlotte. The spirit slipped inside her body. Charlotte gasped, falling to her knees.

Niall went to the ground beside her, holding her. "Charlotte?"

His brothers gathered around them. Charlotte couldn't speak as she fought the spirit taking hold. She lifted her hand, still clutching the potion. She tried to open it but couldn't coordinate her movements. Niall did it for her, and Charlotte opened her mouth, indicating she wanted to drink it.

Niall didn't hesitate. He poured the liquid into her mouth.

As she swallowed, Helena reappeared, jerking out of her body.

Euann and Iain tried to help Charlotte up. "Get her out of here," Niall ordered.

"*How?*" Helena howled, clutching her stomach as she doubled over in pain. "The gaps within you are filled!"

"I am not you," Charlotte croaked. "I found my lost memories. Niall helped me. He tried to help you, too, but you wouldn't let him."

Helena began to scream. Blue flames erupted

over her translucent skin. They grew, consuming her completely. Charlotte covered her ears.

In an instant, the flames died, filtering to the sky in blue smoke.

Charlotte dropped her hands. Iain and Euann let go of her arms. Niall rushed to her side, catching her as she wobbled on unsteady legs.

"Is it over?" she asked.

"Aye. Ya set her free," Niall said. "What was in that potion?"

"I don't know, but Angus told me I'd know when to use it," she said.

Niall held Charlotte closer, and had no intention of ever letting her go. Rocks hit the ground, and they watched as the statue crumbled to a pile of pebbles at their feet.

Chapter Twenty-One

"I would take it all back if I could. I would rewind time if it would fix the future. I would let ya see the truth if that meant ya would look at me once the way I see ya every day."

Charlotte opened her eyes, hearing the words clearly, as if they had just been said. She finally remembered all of it, every moment. Niall had said that to her long before she knew he liked her. Each time he cared for her after her insanity took her too far. He had said that. He had begged for her forgiveness and revealed the depth of his feelings when he thought she couldn't hear.

She was in Niall's bed in the mansion, the room empty. She wasn't sure what she was going to say or do, only that she needed to find him. She wore pajama pants and a shirt borrowed from Malina. The clothes fit her better than Niall's.

She hurried out onto the landing, peering over the stairs. "Niall?"

"Charlotte?" Lydia appeared below her in the front hall.

"Where's Niall? I have to talk to him." Charlotte hurried down the stairs.

"You can't come down here yet," Lydia said, waving her hands that Charlotte should get back.

Charlotte ignored her. "Niall!"

Firelight caught her attention in the dining room. There was a flurry of movement as she entered. Niall stood in a dress shirt as his father tried to thrust a tuxedo jacket at him.

"Ya were supposed to stop her," Margareta gasped, motioning at Lydia to get Charlotte even though it was too late.

"Niall, I needed to see you!" Charlotte rushed toward him. He looked surprised to see her. He glanced around the room as if unsure what to do. Flowers were strewn over a table. Margareta lifted her hand, lighting the candles that had been scattered throughout the room.

"Charlotte..." Niall cleared his throat.

"I love you," Charlotte blurted. "I had to tell you. I know that you love me, too."

"Ah," Lydia said softly. "That's so sweet."

"You're not supposed to be down here yet." Angus again thrust the tuxedo jacket at his son.

"What's going on?" Charlotte asked. Niall clearly wasn't a tuxedo kind of guy and none of the others were dressed up. "Why are you...?" She took the jacket from him and laid it on the back of a chair. "Niall, what's going on here?"

Niall cleared his throat as if he had practiced what he was going to say. His phone beeped and he glanced down, ignoring it. "Charlotte, I have come to realize that..."

"My life has no meaning without ya in it," Margareta whispered.

"My life has no..." He cleared his throat again and took a deep breath. "Ah, dammit, Charlotte. I'm sorry. I know ya deserve a man who can give ya everything, but I love ya and I don't want to live another day without ya. If ya could stand a man who doesn't talk as much as ya might want him to, eats too many fried foods, rides a motorcycle, and fights the occasional demon, then I'd like to be that guy."

"What the hell kind of proposal is that?"

Margareta asked no one in particular. "It's nothing like we practiced."

Niall's phone beeped again.

"Niall, if you can stand a stubborn, occasionally insane, pain-in-the-ass woman, then yes, I would love to be your wife." Charlotte threw her arms around his neck and kissed him. She knew in that moment, everything was perfect. This is where she was meant to be.

"I give up," Margareta said. "Ya two are perfect for each other."

His phone beeped yet again.

Charlotte pulled back. "Maybe you should answer that."

Niall reached into his pocket and kept ahold of her as he pulled up the text so she could see it. "Murdoch said the water sprite migration has taken a turn for the worse. He needs help."

"Water sprites?" Charlotte asked, grinning "Can we go?"

"Ya want to hunt water sprites with me?" Niall asked.

She nodded. "Hell yeah I do. We already took out a wraith, how hard can sprites be?"

Niall grinned. "My bike is parked out front.

We can swing by the apartment and grab some clothes if ya like."

"Perfect," Charlotte nodded. She stopped to hug Lydia. "I'll call you later."

"You better," Lydia said.

"Why does Niall get everything?" Rory teased in a pouty voice, coming from the kitchen. "First he gets the giant pet lizard. Now he gets the girl."

"You have a lizard?" Charlotte asked, not remembering any pets in Niall's apartment. "Do we need to have someone come by and feed it or something?"

"Ah, Nessie is an independent girl," Niall dismissed. "She's fine. But that reminds me." He turned to his cousin. "Rory, I need ya to go take care of the *gremain* in my building. Thanks."

"But..." Rory protested.

Niall ushered Charlotte toward the front door. As they walked outside, she could barely contain her excitement. "I love you so much, Niall. I can't believe it's taken us so long to get here."

He paused by his motorcycle, grinning. "All I have is yours, Charlotte, now and for eternity—my magick, my life, my love. Together, we will live for hundreds of years."

Charlotte arched a brow. "How does that work?"

"My power will infuse ya with my life and my immortality will become yours." He kissed her softly before straddling his bike. He snapped his fingers, materialized a helmet for her. "That doesn't give ya second thoughts, does it?"

"Not for a second." Charlotte slipped the helmet over her head and climbed on behind him. The motor revved between her legs, sending a shiver through her. She grinned, feeling strangely warm for such a cool day. He took off down the hill, speeding them to their future.

Chapter Twenty-Two

EPILOGUE

Oregon Coast, Two Weeks Later...

If someone had told Charlotte that one day she'd be staying in an RV in the Oregon coastal woods, she would have laughed herself silly. Then again, if that same person would have told her she'd be engaged to Niall MacGregor and happier than she'd ever been in her life, she would have had them committed.

Yet, here she was, sitting at the small booth table gazing out at the dark ocean. Glints of moon-light defined the waves. She had a feeling Niall would have camped out by his motorcycle if not for her. Charlotte liked to think she brought a bit of domestication to his life, while he brought an adventure to hers.

"*Fíorghrá*," Niall said as he opened the door. She heard the electric motor of the steps automatically lower them to the ground. "It's time."

Charlotte grabbed her jacket and went to join him. He held out his hand to help her out of the vehicle. He shut the door, and the steps retracted.

Niall kept hold of her hand as he led her down a sandy path toward the water. The cool wind whipped his hair around his head. She felt her heart beat faster as she followed him. It didn't matter where they were, what they were doing, as long as she was next to him she felt complete.

"Where is Murdoch?" she asked as they neared the water. He led her around a fallen log someone had moved to create a seat near a barren fire pit. Her feet slipped in the loose sand with each step.

"Down the beach," Niall gestured into the distance. "He'll change the water sprites' course and send them our direction."

A small shiver of excitement traveled over her as the anticipation built. They stopped near the water's edge. The wet sand created a firmer path.

"Don't be nervous," he whispered.

"I'm not," Charlotte answered. After Helena, a few water sprites hardly seemed terrifying.

It started with a soft glow in the distance, the

gliding of lights in the water. The sprites swam along the shoreline, some bumping along the shallow water so that their heads surfaced. Lips parted each time to release a gentle screech. Though their legs and arms did not move, they had the shape of humans being pulled in currents. Bioluminescent skin radiated the color of blue moonlight. More sprites followed the first until hundreds gathered along the shoreline like a pod of glowing dolphins.

Niall lifted his hands toward the water. She saw his lips move but did not hear his words. Threads of magick wove from his hands toward the ocean. He directed it toward the leaders of the pod, sending them back toward the ocean. After a few moments, he dropped his magick and sighed.

"They should go back into the deep waters for another hundred years." Niall reached for her to pull her next to him.

"What happens if they crash on the shore? Do they attack humans?" Charlotte watched the beautiful sight as the sprites moved past them.

"No, they'd die," Niall said. "Most supernaturals do not pose a threat to humans. Often, it is the other way around. That's why we send them back out to sea. If one was to beach themselves and humans found the remains, the hunt would be on."

Charlotte slipped her arm behind his waist and angled her body toward his. She cupped his cheek, bringing him to her for a brief kiss. "This has to be one of the most romantic dates I've ever been on, Mr. MacGregor."

He grinned. "Ya wouldn't prefer candlelight dinners at some fancy hotel?"

She shook her head as she once again looked out at the glowing water. "Candlelight has nothing on this."

"I love ya, Charlotte," Niall whispered. "All that I am, and have, is yours."

"Then I'd say life is pretty damn good," she answered just as softly. "I love you, too, Niall."

The End

The Series Continues...

WARLOCKS MACGREGOR 6: KISSES AND CURSES

Scottish Warlock Euann MacGregor may be the tech savvy one in his family, but when it comes to love, savvy doesn't enter into the equation. So when he crosses paths, in the most unusual way, with a woman who holds an essential piece to a puzzle that has haunted the MacGregor family for decades, he's torn between wanting answers and wanting her. Forces beyond his control have brought them together, but those same dangers might also be what tears them apart forever.

Warning: Contains yummy, hot, mischievous MacGregors who are almost certainly up to no good

Warlocks MacGregor® 6: Kisses and Curses
Chapter One Excerpt

Green Vallis, Wisconsin

"If anyone cares, Uncle Raibeart is naked in the back gardens." Euann glanced up from the security feed on his laptop. Two of his brothers and their cousin, Rory, sat at the formal dining table with him. A trail of light made its way in from the window, creeping across the room to mark the movement of time.

Rory leaned to look lazily past a large flower vase in the middle of the table. He shook his head in denial at Euann. Rory appeared more interested in his coffee cup than anything else. "Not unless the giant puppy I've been trying to get Malina and Jane to materialize for me is chasing him."

"Ah..." Euann squinted and leaned closer to the screen. "No, it looks like...*gremains,* maybe?"

Rory waved his hand in dismissal. "He's probably trying to get one to marry him. Let Raibeart have his shot at love."

"Can ya imagine the children that would come from that union?" Iain mused. His brother's feet were kicked up on the table and he picked at a croissant, throwing more pieces onto the plate than into his mouth.

"Should we go rid the gardens of the creatures once and for all?" Euann asked, even as he lacked the motivation to do so.

"It's too early to deal with *gremains*," Iain dismissed, suppressing a yawn. "Let's do it tomorrow."

"I don't want to break up Raibeart's date," their oldest brother, Erik, added. He didn't look up from the thriller he read on his smartphone. "He'll scream if he needs help."

A melancholy air had settled over the MacGregor estate, like a mist covering the mansion and surrounding grounds that would not dissipate. The entire family felt it, well, at least those of warlock blood.

The twenty-fifth anniversary of Kenneth's disappearance was upon them, and they were no closer to having answers than they had been the night he'd gone missing.

They all had theories—vortex to another world, fairy ring to another realm, magick gone awry, causing Kenneth to lose his corporeal form, evil spells, statue potions, witch hunters. Erik had convinced himself Kenneth left of his own accord and didn't want to be found. Otherwise they would have had a hint of his whereabouts. No one else really believed that. Kenneth would not do that to the family. For a time, his brother Niall had thought maybe a nest of vampires had taken him, but that turned out to be a dead lead. The family had tried seances and spells, summonings and incantations, offerings and prayers. Nothing brought Kenneth back.

Every year, his parents, Angus and Margareta MacGregor, would go to West Virginia, where Kenneth was last located by a credit card receipt at a local bar. What started as a pilgrimage of hope had slowly turned into a bleak journey they were compelled to continue.

Euann missed his brother and felt the hole that had been left behind in their lives. It was an ache that would not lessen. He supposed it would be worse for parents, losing a child and never having an answer as to what had happened to him. It didn't matter that Kenneth had been just over four hundred years old at the time. To parents, their child would always be their child.

In the course of a warlock's lifetime, twenty-five years wasn't a lot of time, but it was enough to lose hope, to accept the hollow feeling might never go away. It had become a darkened part of their souls.

Euann realized he watched Raibeart on the security feed of the back gardens without really seeing him. He flinched and then jumped back in his seat. "Och, that's not right. Raibeart is doing tai chi."

"What self-respecting warlock uses technology instead of magick for security? There are only six acres of gardens. Ya should be able to cover that with a couple of protection spells." Erik still didn't look up from his book. "I think it's because the sack man forgot to give ya true magick when he tricked ma into taking ya from him."

His brothers always teased him about being the son of a sack man and not a real MacGregor. It was an old joke, one they had not given up since childhood. They liked to claim the Spanish boogeyman fathered him, and that is why he wasn't a true Scottish warlock. Euann hated golf and whiskey, which his family loved, and preferred playing with gadgets instead of using a magickal solution.

Euann arched a brow and, without verbally answering Erik's insult, he pulled open a file on his computer and sent a video to all of his family's cellphones. Seconds later, Rory's phone dinged, Iain's beeped, and Erik frowned before sweeping his finger over his screen to ignore the notification so he could keep reading.

Rory glanced at Euann with a questioning look.

Euann just gave him a half-smile and kept idly checking the camera feeds around the property.

"Ly-di-ah!" As Rory played the video, the sound of Erik singing to woo his now-wife belted out of the phone.

Barely a second later, Iain's phone joined their cousin's creating a slightly out of sync playback of the song. *"Ly-di-ah! I sit beneath your window, laaaass, singing 'cause I loooove your aaaass."*

Erik sat forward in his seat as he swiped his finger to look at the message he'd disregarded moments before.

"Ly-di-ah!"

"Dammit, Euann!" Erik swore.

"Ly-di-ah!"

"Ohmigod, there's dancing," Rory exclaimed, slapping his hand on the table and gasping for breath through his amusement.

"Those are some sweet moves, brother," Iain added, shaking his hips back and forth in his chair.

As if on cue, Rory and Iain belted out with the recording, *"Ly-di-ah!"*

"Turn it off," Erik demanded.

"Ly-di-ah! Ya smell just like a, uh, la-ven-der-ah mint, and I think I like your scent."

"Och, brother, ya cannot carry a tune." Iain set his phone down and plugged his ears with his fingers. "Ya do not do the MacGregor name proud."

Erik gestured his hand toward Iain, material-izing a stiff breeze that sent Iain's phone flying into the dining room wall. It crashed so hard that it stopped playing.

"Ya didn't have to do that," Iain protested.

"Erik!"

The sound of his wife's voice caused Erik to stiffen and look around as if he suspected he was in trouble. It was still the recording.

"Uh-oh, Lydia sounds annoyed." Iain picked up his broken phone. "I don't think she liked your song."

"Yes, my lavender," the recording of Erik's voice said. Rory and Iain laughed harder.

"Malina drugged me," Erik protested. It was true. Their sister had helped Lydia make a love potion as a prank and it backfired, horribly. It had caused Erik to become obsessed with his true love to the point of being dangerous. He'd called a storm that nearly destroyed the whole town, and he'd even shifted into a monstrous version of his puma form.

"Don't call me lavender," Lydia's recording stated firmly. Rory turned his phone so Iain could also appreciate the way Erik groveled.

"Yes, my rose."

"Don't call me rose."

"Yes, my—"

The video clip ended when Erik walked out of the frame of the security camera. Iain and Rory doubled over with laughter.

"Ly-di-ah!" Iain sang, placing his hand on his heart as he crooned toward Rory.

"Ly-di-ah!" Rory returned louder than his cousin.

"I will not forget this," Erik told Euann. "It's going in the revenge book."

Euann wasn't worried. "File it under the section called, I'm not scared of the kitty cat's threats."

Erik marched toward the main foyer.

"Oh, wait, Erik, we're sorry," Rory said as Erik reached the door.

"Yeah, come back." Iain moved around the side

of the table to follow his brother, with Rory right behind him.

Erik stopped and arched a skeptical brow as he turned.

As if reading each other's minds, both Rory and Iain began bouncing around the dining room, lifting their arms and kicking their legs in a bad rendition of an already hilarious dance as they mocked Erik.

"Oh, Ly-di-ah, my lavender cake," Iain sang.

"How I love to make ya quake," Rory added.

"Kill me for heaven's sake," Iain continued, shaking his ass violently so the kilt he wore shook back and forth. He winked at Erik. "They call this twerking. Try it next time. Might help."

Erik lifted his finger and pointed it deliberately at Euann. Under his breath, he uttered, "Revenge."

Euann laughed and, as Erik strode from the room, he called, "Wait, lavender boy, I have more. Don't ya want to see...?" He let his words trail off. He heard Erik's boots hitting heavily on the stairs as he headed toward his bedroom. There, Erik kept a magick mirror that would transport him home to the Victorian mansion he shared with Lydia.

The teasing had lightened the mood of the morning. Iain and Rory went back to their chairs.

Euann knew it wouldn't last but for now they were smiling.

"Do ya know who would have loved that?" Iain asked, only to answer his own question. "Kenneth."

And with that, the mood dampened.

Rory nodded as he sat back down by his coffee. "Yeah, he really would have."

About Michelle M. Pillow

New York Times & *USA TODAY* Bestselling Author

Michelle loves to travel and try new things, whether it's a paranormal investigation of an old Vaudeville Theatre or climbing Mayan temples in Belize. She believes life is an adventure fueled by copious amounts of coffee.

Newly relocated to the American South, Michelle is involved in various film and documentary projects with her talented director husband. She is mom to a fantastic artist. And she's managed by a dog and cat who make sure she's meeting her deadlines.

For the most part she can be found wearing pajama pants and working in her office. There may or may not be dancing. It's all part of the creative process.

~

**Come say hello! Michelle loves talking
with readers on social media!**

www.MichellePillow.com

f facebook.com/AuthorMichellePillow

y twitter.com/michellepillow

O instagram.com/michellempillow

BB bookbub.com/authors/michelle-m-pillow

g goodreads.com/Michelle_Pillow

a amazon.com/author/michellepillow

▶ youtube.com/michellepillow

P pinterest.com/michellepillow

Complimentary Material

Curses and Cupcakes

A COZY PARANORMAL MYSTERY

Exclusive First Chapter Excerpt

Curses and Cupcakes
by Michelle M. Pillow

*Welcome to Everlasting, Maine, where there's no
such thing as normal.*

Marcy Lewis is cursed (honestly and truly) which
makes dating very interesting. With a string of loser
boyfriends behind her, she's done looking for love
in all the wrong places. That is until the new fire-
fighter arrives in the sleepy seaside town of Everlasting. Nicholas Logan is unlike any other man

she's ever had in her life. When someone starts sending her photographs that raise a red flag it soon becomes apparent that she's not just cursed, she's in serious danger.

Nicholas doesn't know what to make of the charismatic young woman managing the local coffee shop. As a string of mysterious fires begin popping up around town, the two unite in search of clues as to who or what is responsible, discovering along the way that things are very rarely what they seem to be.

~

Exclusive First Chapter Excerpt

Everlasting, Maine

Marcy Lewis collected engagement rings like other women collected designer purses. She didn't do it on purpose, and it wasn't anything she bragged about. What woman would brag about being cursed to have her heart broken over and over again? It wasn't that she merely had bad luck with men or only dated bad boys and made horrible choices. That would have been too easy. That she could have hired a therapist to deal with.

No, she was honestly and truly cursed.

Marcy was doomed to become whatever the man in her life thought he wanted, transforming her physical appearance and the dominant parts of her personality. If the man liked artists, the fact she had wanted to be the next Picasso in the third grade would emerge. If the man wanted an accountant, she found herself up in the middle of the night reading tax code. One man had a thing for the rodeo. Thank the heavens there had not been any nearby at the time, or she might have found herself on the wrong side of a bull.

Marcy slipped an engagement ring off her finger and set it on the bathroom sink. The relationships always ended poorly. That was what had happened the night before. She came home from work to find her house in shambles. Her recent ex, Donnie Huff, had taken everything of value he could find. She would have called to report it, but the police wouldn't get anything back, and trying would only prolong the suffering.

"Hello, officer," she mumbled sarcastically, "I'm cursed, and my ex stole my collection of engagement rings. Can you please go arrest him for being a jerk?"

A grumpy meow answered her as if protesting her sour mood.

"Point taken, Mr. Monty," Marcy answered the cat as she went to peek into her disheveled bedroom. "At least he did not take what is most valuable."

Her two cats were the most valuable things Marcy had. Life mattered more than objects any day of the week, and she'd give a thousand engagement rings to make sure her cats were safe.

Mr. Monty the Spectacular stared at her accusingly from his perch on an overturned dresser drawer. He'd somehow worked his way into one of her bra straps and wore it like a belt. She'd adopted him from the local shelter, but he looked to have the pedigree of a British Shorthair, with his hefty build, thick coat, and broad features. His bi-color fur was mostly blue-gray, except for the triangle of white starting at a point between his eyes, widening down his cheeks and covering his two front paws. Marcy crossed over to him and pulled the bra off. When she'd finished, there appeared to be an air of disappointment in his copper gaze.

Hiding somewhere was his best friend, Mr. Whiffle Pot Hopscotch the Magnificent, a white and orange longhair with small ears that bent forward and down toward the front of the head like the Scottish Fold breed. The two of them enjoyed staring out of the window and tapping the glass anytime a kid walked by. Marcy couldn't tell if they wanted to play, or if they were two grumpy men yelling at the children to get off the lawn.

Strewn clothes and treasured ornaments covered the floor like they'd been tossed in a chaos salad, and then abruptly discarded for better prospects elsewhere. Her home décor wasn't fancy, but it had been her haven, kitschy and cool, held together by craft wire and luck. An antique tin sign advertising soda pointed up from a nest of T-shirts on the floor. Her favorite piece of furniture, an old wooden park bench, lay in two pieces as if it had been stomped in half.

Marcy went back to the bathroom mirror to watch the flower tattoos on her arms fade as if they had never been there. In an hour, they'd be gone. At least she hadn't endured pain at the hands of a tattooist to get them. The body art had appeared as suddenly as it left, and soon what she had worn as a badge of her commitment would disappear into her private mental trove of mistakes along with her other errors in judgment. In two hours, her hair would be a lighter shade of brown and the nose piercing would close, and in three hours no one would remember the last incarnation of Marcy Lewis except in pictures they would assume were costumes.

As a bonus, anytime she tried to tell people she was cursed, they looked at her like she was talking gibberish. The curse really did cover everything— no one saw the changes, she couldn't tell people what was going on, and she was made to go through it alone with no ending in sight.

Marcy wondered what kind of person she would become next. "How long do you think it will last this time, Monty, being blessedly single before I find my next heartbreak and lose myself again?"

She leaned to look at him through the bathroom door. Monty had wiggled his way back into the bra strap and now licked his paw as he groomed himself.

"You are one strange cat."

Monty lifted his leg and kept licking.

"I don't suppose you have seen my phone in this mess, have you?" Marcy knew the cat was notorious for lying on top of anything small and electronic—TV remotes, phones, even the electric wine opener a friend had given her one year for

Christmas. Marcy swept her finger under him and found her phone. "Thanks, Monty."

Aside from a few social-media notifications and a call from her mother, no one had tried to get ahold of her. Marcy placed the phone on her dresser, trying to ignore the mess Donnie had made of her room, and went to find clothes to get ready for work. She looked at the tight T-shirts hanging in the closet like someone peeking in at a memory of what used to be her favorite. Her clothing choices read like the wardrobe of a theater troupe—relaxed chick, motorcycle old lady, naughty librarian, not-so-naughty librarian, sweater-vested schoolmarm, tax accountant, tattooed creative...

None of them felt like her true self, but they were all versions.

All it took was a mutual attraction, and she lost part of herself. She became someone else's ideal, until she didn't know who she was anymore.

There was enough artist left in her to make her pick a blue T-shirt, distressed blue jeans, and a pea coat for work. It wasn't glamorous, but working at Witch's Brew Coffee Shop and Bakery in Everlasting, Maine, was her idea of solid employment. She had been trying to make her way through college with online classes, but it was hard going when a relationship always seemed to throw a wrench into the works. Maybe the next guy would like educated girls who dedicated themselves to getting ahead. That would make for a nice change.

The longest she'd been single was three months. Of course, she hadn't left her house much during that time, but it had been a glorious three months. Maybe she'd get lucky and no one would fancy her.

Maybe she could stop showering.

Or shaving.

Or brushing her hair.

Never mind. With her luck, she'd attract some hoarder who wanted her to live on top of a stack of newspapers from the 1970s.

There was the secret hope that someone, somehow, would have the answers she needed. This was Everlasting after all. Strange things happened here every day. The unofficial town motto was, "Everlasting, where there is no such thing as normal." To an outsider, it looked like a thriving fishing village steeped in New England culture. In reality, it was a safe harbor for supernatural creatures. It was why she'd moved from her hometown of Nickerson, Maine.

"Feel free to clean up while I'm gone," Marcy

told Mr. Monty as she grabbed her purse and phone. He gave a dismissive meow and continued licking himself. "See you later, Whiffle." Whiffle Pot did not deign to give her an answer.

The walk to work from her rental house was only a few blocks, which made the expense of owning a car unnecessary. Except for some strange happenings and untimely deaths during the Cranberry Festival, the town was relatively safe. Well, mostly...sort of.

She sighed heavily. This breakup wasn't so bad. Donnie wasn't her soul mate. She knew that. Betrayal hurt more than anything, but the sting was already lessening.

The irony was the only time she felt normal was after a breakup. Those parts of her that these men summoned to the surface cared for them, enough to create a fake kind of love. Perhaps not true love, but a worthy imitation of it. She'd tried to stop it, but the curse always found her. The curse always won.

Marcy searched her phone out of habit. Her mother hadn't left a message, so Marcy sent her a text telling her she was on her way to work and would call her later. Social media provided a mild distraction on her walk. A few authors and celebrities posted clever quips about life, and some guy who claimed to have gone to her high school commented randomly on a photo of the latte art she'd created the other day.

"Thanks, Henry Franklin Jones," she mumbled reading his name and politely liking his comment. He and a few others appeared on her profile like being from the same hometown made them buddies. She honestly didn't even remember going to school with many of the people who commented. When she thought of high school, she remembered breaking her leg, working so hard for most of it only to barely graduate, and disappointing her parents' hopes for her future. The curse had started her senior year with Joey Zimmerman and it had been downhill from there.

The sound of a siren broke through her thoughts as a fire truck shot from around a corner and headed away from Main Street. Marcy automatically lifted her eyes to watch as it passed. Firefighters were like soldiers. Slap a uniform on a man, and there was something more attractive about him. She lifted her hand in greeting, but light reflected off the window to hide the driver in a passing flash. A trail of smoke lifted into the distant sky.

Marcy quickened her pace. She worked in the historic downtown district. A giant oak tree marked her turn onto Main Street. Whenever she walked past it, she touched it for luck. She had no reason to believe it would actually work, other than it was old and pretty and she always imagined that the tree would have borne witness to a great many things.

All the festival decorations had been taken down. The town felt empty with the October tourists gone, and the streets were not as bright and cheery with the giant cranberry sculptures back into storage until next year.

Seabirds flew overhead. Fall leaves littered the ground and the air felt cooler. Marcy pulled at the lapels of her pea coat to keep the breeze off her neck. Snow was coming. She could sense it in the air.

Witch's Brew Coffee Shop and Bakery was everything a small-town coffee shop should be. Mismatched chairs and heirloom tables seemingly scattered in a haphazard fashion over a painted concrete floor, gave it a sense of homeliness. Worn patterns from foot traffic only endorsed the hospitable feel of the place.

Marcy's boss was a witch, or more correctly she was a witch-in-denial. Anna Crawford didn't use her magical gifts. She preferred to do things normally. At first, Marcy had hoped that Anna could help her break her curse, but her boss didn't like to talk about those kinds of supernatural things. And lately, Anna had been preoccupied with her relationship with investigative journalist, Jackson Argent.

Aunt Polly ran a small magic store in the back storage room of the coffee shop named, Polly's Perfectly Magical Mystical Wondrous World of Wonders. It was a big name for a tiny store. Though she was Anna's blood relation, everyone called her Aunt Polly. She was a special sort of person. She genuinely cared about people but didn't care what anyone thought about her eccentricities.

Polly had no qualms about being a witch, or about marching to her own offbeat drum. However, the spells she cast often went awry. The woman had forced Hugh Lupine into wolf form and had, if rumors held true, given him fleas. Marcy didn't believe that last part. Hugh was always well groomed.

Marcy had seen firsthand how Polly bestowed a rainbow comb-over on a customer. Jerry still came in for blueberry muffins several times a week and, to be honest, he was pretty proud of those new hairs.

Then there was Herman, Polly's pet lobster who had to be enchanted. Otherwise, Marcy couldn't explain how Polly had managed to dress him in a sailor suit for pictures...or why it had looked like the lobster actually enjoyed it. There were more examples of Aunt Polly's spell casting around town, too many to list. Rainbow hair and enchanted crustaceans might be amusing, but they were not the type of help Marcy needed to end a curse.

Everlasting had not turned out to be the miracle cure Marcy had hoped for. At least the people were nice, and she had a steady job with a lenient boss. Plus she'd been given a raise and had been promoted to manager. That was something she could be proud of.

Anna tried to create a welcoming, creative vibe with her oversize couches and comfortable chairs, inviting people to stay and chat. Brick walls and exposed wood beams added to the feel. Anna was a talented photographer, and the walls were deco-rated with photographs of people and places in town. She switched the photo displays at random times. Currently, one showcased the lighthouse standing tall against a dark sky surrounded by cats. Another pictured a waitress whose nametag read "Betsy" as she served blueberry crumble at the Chickadee's Diner. There was also a photograph of Wilber Messing's old hunting cabin on the outskirts of town. It was a strange, dilapidated structure with boards over the windows and no-trespassing signs with warnings like, "Trespassers Won't Be Seen Again."

"Marcy, is that you?" Anna's voice called from the kitchen.

Marcy turned her attention from the photos and shrugged out of her pea coat. "Yeah, it's me." She glanced at her arm. The floral tattoos had faded completely and her skin felt naked without them. She lightly touched her nose where the piercing used to be. Just once she wished someone would notice her physical change and ask about it. Then maybe when she said she was cursed and needed help, they'd understand her.

"The supplier forgot to send the extra baking flour we ordered, so Jackson and I are going to see if we can find enough to last us the rest of this week. It's no Cranberry Festival mad rush, but we have several sizable orders waiting to be filled. The fire station has two recruits and a new hire, so I wanted to send over a welcoming box of something delicious. Not sure what." Anna always spoke with a chaotic grace that amazed Marcy.

"All right," Marcy answered.

Anna continued, "The Sacred Order of Hairy Old Men is hosting a new member drive tomorrow, the hospital staff has a birthday party for one of the doctors on Friday, there are three baby showers, a wedding tea party, a convention needing breakfast croissants for some trust seminar, and if a Dana calls here again begging for a birthday cake, please try to make her understand we're not that kind of bakery, and I wouldn't have the first clue how to make a four-foot teddy bear cake."

"Want me to ask Polly to whip up a bear cake?" Marcy teased. She smiled even though Anna couldn't see it.

"Oh, for the love of sanity, no," Anna exclaimed. "The cake would probably come to life and try to take a bite out of the birthday boy in self-defense." Anna's words became muffled for a moment, before she finished with, "I hate to do this to you, but do you think you can stay late again tonight and help me handle the store? And maybe fit in a few extra hours this week?"

"Not a problem," Marcy answered. The distraction would be welcome.

"You don't have plans with Donnie tonight?"

She took a deep breath. "There is no Donnie."

"What?" Anna came out of the back room. Dark, wavy hair had been wound into a messy bun at the nape of her neck, and curls threatened to spiral out of its hold.

She was in the process of putting on a scarf. The bright red contrasted the dark blue fleece of her sweater. She held her coat in her hand and looked at Marcy for the briefest of seconds like her employee was unfamiliar, and then she blinked slowly as her mind accepted the new appearance. "What happened? Did you breakup?"

Marcy thought about lying, but she liked Anna. She might even dare as much as to say they were friends. "He stole my jewelry and ran off with a woman that he met in the bar two towns over. I don't know which town, but he said it was two over."

"Oh, no, Marcy. Did you report him?"

"It was only costume jewelry," she downplayed. It's not like she wanted to report fifteen stolen engagement rings and eighty-three dollars in cash. That would make for some embarrassing small-town gossip.

"What do you need? Do you need the day off? A gallon of ice cream? A baseball bat and an alibi? I can send Jackson on his own to deal with the flour situation." Anna followed Marcy into the kitchen. "Do you want me to have Polly cast a spell on him to make his hair fall out? Anything you need, name it."

"I think..." Marcy glanced around, trying to figure out how to answer that question. "I think I feel like baking cupcakes. Do you care if we try cupcake varieties in the case this week? I know it's not our usual thing, but..."

The urge to bake was strange, but it had to be all her since she'd not met any men on the walk from her house.

"Go for it. Comfort food. I'll help." Anna hung up her coat and started to reach for the closest white apron. It had the logo of a magical coffee bean screen-printed on the front. It also had Marcy's name written on the strap. "What kind do you want? Candied hazelnut or key lime, or do we go chocolate pudding filled or a ganache or—"

"No, boss, you go with Jackson. I need to work and not think about anything. I'll be fine." Marcy glanced at the empty shop. "Besides, I can handle this crowd."

Anna chuckled. "I haven't turned on the open sign yet. I've been so frazzled by the flour crisis, I forgot."

"That makes sense. I was wondering why we were empty." Marcy took the apron from Anna and looped it over her own head before tying the straps behind her waist. "You go. I have this handled here. I'll make cupcakes for the firefighters and enough to fill the case. Who knows, they might be a hit. And if Dana calls again, I'll tell her it is cupcakes or nothing. If she's that desperate to spend her money here, let her."

"Who doesn't like cupcakes?" Anna said by way of agreement. "Actually, while you're in the mood, the Sacred Order will take whatever goodies we want to bring, so we could take some over there for their new member banquet, as well. That would probably make a nice change to go with the scones."

"Done," Marcy said.

"Call me if anything changes—" Anna placed a gentle hand on her arm, "—or if you want to talk, or yell, or cry, or if you need anything at all. Promise me you will."

Marcy nodded. "Yes, but I'll be fine."

She listened to Anna's footsteps hurry up the stairs to the apartment she shared with Jackson above the shop. Anna and Jackson had only been together for a short time, but Marcy had a feeling the two of them would last. There was something fated about the couple. With so many failed relationships under her belt, Marcy knew a good one when she saw it.

Curses and Cupcakes - Now available!

MichellePillow.com

Please Leave a Review

THANK YOU FOR READING!

Please take a moment to share your thoughts by reviewing this book.

Be sure to check out Michelle's other titles at www.MichellePillow.com

9 781625 011688